"Did you try to radio for help?"

He nodded. "Couldn't get through."

"Isaiah, what if he'd caught you?" Heidi crawled closer to him in the tent. "He'll kill you if he finds out."

He started to speak but she pressed her hand over his mouth. "Don't say he's going to kill us anyway. I don't want to hear it. There has to be another way... Why don't we overpower them, get the guns back. Something." She hated the trembling that crept into her voice along with rising panic.

"If we get the chance, we will. But I need to tell you something." He gripped her shoulders. "I found the missing gang member's body yesterday."

Covering her mouth, she sobbed softly. Isaiah pulled her to him and held her. His arms felt strong around her.

"Heidi, he might not be the last person to die as we make it through these mountains. Do you understand what I'm saying?"

She nodded. The harsh environment would pick them off, one by one. Then maybe they could worry about fighting whoever was left. But she didn't get the chance to voice her thoughts on his words.

Outside the tent, gunfire resounded through the icy mountains.

Elizabeth Goddard is an award-winning author of over twenty novels, including the romantic mystery, *The Camera Never Lies*–winner of a prestigious Carol Award in 2011. After acquiring her computer science degree, she worked at a software firm before eventually retiring to raise her four children and become a professional writer. In addition to writing, she homeschools her children and serves with her husband in ministry.

Books by Elizabeth Goddard

Love Inspired Suspense

Freezing Point
Treacherous Skies
Riptide
Wilderness Peril

Mountain Cove Series

Buried
Untraceable

Visit the Author Profile page at Harlequin.com

UNTRACEABLE

ELIZABETH GODDARD

HARLEQUIN® LOVE INSPIRED® SUSPENSE

Recycling programs
for this product may
not exist in your area.

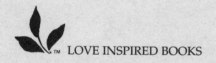

LOVE INSPIRED BOOKS

ISBN-13: 978-0-373-67668-2

Untraceable

www.Harlequin.com

Printed in U.S.A.

For his anger lasts only a moment, but his favor lasts a lifetime; weeping may stay for the night, but rejoicing comes in the morning.
—*Psalms* 30:5

This story is dedicated to search and rescue teams everywhere, to men and women who volunteer their time, money and skills and willingly place themselves in danger to find and rescue complete strangers. And of course, all my stories are dedicated to my family—my three sons, Christopher, Jonathan and Andrew, and my daughter, Rachel (and new son-in-law, Richard), and my husband, Dan—for giving me the time and space I need to create new worlds and characters. You guys rock!

Acknowledgments

Writers don't work in a vacuum, especially if they're novelists. I couldn't write without the encouragement and support I receive from my writing buddies—Lisa Harris, Shannon McNear and Lynette Sowell, and many more—so glad God brought us together on this writing journey!

I'd also like to thank my friends in Juneau who provided me with invaluable material regarding specific information—Doug Wessen, a community leader and SAR hero extraordinaire. And thanks to Teresa, a writing friend in Juneau who works for the US Forest Service. You're always available with just the right answer or photograph. Thanks to Bill Glude of the Alaska Avalanche Center for his assistance, and for training search and rescue volunteers. Any mistakes are mine alone either by accident or on purpose in taking artistic license to create a more adventurous and appealing story world.

ONE

"Off rappel!"

Heidi adjusted her night vision goggles at her brother Cade's call up the rocky cliff face from below. The snow-covered, mountainous landscape looked green and black, but at least she could see instead of stumbling around in the dark and falling to her death. Even though the moon was out in full force, this side of the mountain remained in the shadows.

The helicopter had dropped them off as close as possible to the summit, but they'd still had to hike another two hours to get to the place where they would rappel down to the trapped climbers, at least one of them injured, or so the three rescuers—Heidi and Cade Warren and Isaiah Callahan—had been informed.

As a member of North Face Mountain Search and Rescue—like the other Warren siblings—this was only the second time Heidi had climbed at night, and she shoved aside the unpleasant memory of the first. There was enough tension between her and her brother Cade, and unfortunately their friend and coworker Isaiah—who usually flew the helicopter—that she didn't need to tack on anything more to an already heavy load. And it wasn't just the emotional and mental burden. The pack on her back weighed her down, too.

Drawing in a cold breath, she hoisted the hefty pack—loaded down with climbing, medical and camping gear for spending the night—and rappelled the cliff. Cade, ever the protective brother, had insisted on going first, though Heidi was the trained technical climber of the three.

She'd made it halfway to the next rap station and paused for a rest, when gunfire ricocheted off the mountain. Heidi jerked and lost her balance. Her overfilled pack pulled her over, flipflopping her. Now hanging upside down, her heart pounded.

She was the technical climber here.

She was the expert they counted on to assist in getting these people out.

She hadn't wanted to come. Not after what had happened last summer. But there'd been no choice. Two other daunting rescue operations were ongoing and they needed the manpower. If only she weren't out of practice.

All her fault. This was on her, and she knew it.

Heidi was a wreck, but she couldn't afford to give in to her emotions right now. Those climbers stranded in the saddle between the summits couldn't afford her messing up.

No way would she call for help, though. The last thing Cade and Isaiah needed was a rescuer who required rescuing. Besides, she'd assured Cade she could do this, but even if she hadn't, he'd pretty much insisted that she try. Isaiah had been the one to protest. He hadn't wanted her here. Whether because he personally didn't want to work with her after distancing himself for some unknown reason or because he didn't trust her abilities, she wasn't sure. Either way, his attitude stabbed her like an ice ax.

"What's going on up there, Heidi?" Cade asked over the radio.

"Nothing."

"You need help?" Now Isaiah. Great.

And the incident command center would hear their conversation, too. Over the years, they'd developed their own radio-speak, and didn't use the more technical terms. Cade always wanted them to talk plainly. Worked for her.

"Heidi, I asked if you're good?" Isaiah again.

At the very least, she would prove to Isaiah she was back. She could do this. "I'm rapping down. You're distracting me."

With all the strength she could muster, she

grabbed the rope and inched her way up, righting herself. Then she breathed a sigh of relief.

But what about the gunfire she'd heard? Heidi used her night vision goggles to scan the mountain and the saddle below, but saw nothing of concern. Was it someone chasing off a bear somewhere? Cade and Isaiah hadn't mentioned it. Had she imagined it? Or was it simply echoing from miles away? She wouldn't bring it up. All she needed was for them to think she was hearing things. As always, Isaiah and Cade were packing weapons in case they came across a bear, so she wouldn't worry.

Following Cade down, she rappelled, careful that the unusually heavy pack wouldn't throw her off balance again. She met him at the second rappel. A glance down revealed a beaming flashlight and a small fire burning nearly four hundred feet below.

Voices resounded from the camp. The climbers must have spotted their rescuers. Cade rappelled again. Heidi watched and waited before she followed. She glanced up but couldn't see Isaiah from here. He was likely growing impatient to hear her call.

Heidi looked down at Cade and saw him swinging over, creating a new path.

"Be careful. There's a vertical ice wall and a sheer drop," Cade told them over the radio.

Negotiating the terrain would be difficult enough under the circumstances, but with the expected inclement weather, even in April, things could only get worse.

"Off rappel," Cade called.

Heidi clipped in and called up, repeating the words to Isaiah, and they were back in rhythm, rappelling and descending a snow-covered slope in the middle of a cold, wintry night.

Reaching the vertical ice wall Cade had warned about, she secured her harness and traversed the cliff face, following Cade's lead. She found the third rappel station and called up to Isaiah before descending the rest of the way.

The saddle where the two summits met formed a wind tunnel. Maybe that's why Cade hadn't mentioned the gunfire. He hadn't even heard it. The high-pitched wail of the wind harmonized with deeper tones making Heidi think of a lost lover singing a seriously morbid screamo song. Thank goodness she'd grown out of that phase a decade ago.

Dropping a few feet to the ground, the pack pulled Heidi back and she fell on her rear.

Thankfully, in this spot, the curve in the rock formations above and around them protected them from the harsh blasts of arctic gusts. She hoped that would remain the case.

"You okay?" Cade offered his hand.

She didn't take it, but instead slipped from the pack. "That thing is too heavy."

"I hear you," he said.

Isaiah joined them. He tugged Heidi around to face him, his touch surprising her. She tried to ignore the current coursing through his gloved hand and her parka to burn the skin on her arm. It was the first time he'd come close to acting as if he cared in months.

Still wearing his night vision goggles, he looked her up and down. "You okay?"

"Of course, I'm fine. We're here to help them." Heidi pointed at the group who remained huddled next to their small fire, a couple of them standing, expectantly looking in the direction of the rescuers. "Stop worrying about me."

She couldn't take his attention on her right now. It only confused her and she needed to focus. Besides, she hated to be coddled, and Cade's and Isaiah's concern was too much. Cade was right to insist she had to get back into search and rescue now or she never would, but after what happened, after she'd been part of a jaunt in the mountains with friends that ended in tragedy, Heidi second-guessed everything she did. Succeeding tonight in this rescue would serve as a rescue for Heidi, in a way. And she prayed that her participation wasn't a mistake, that it wouldn't cost more lives. She reminded herself that North Face needed her today.

Heidi helped Cade and Isaiah gather up their packs and equipment so they wouldn't end up buried in the snow once the storm set in. By the look of the dark clouds rushing in from the west, they didn't have much time. She led the way, hiking over to the climbers hunkered by the fire about a hundred yards in the distance. With a glance back she saw Cade and Isaiah pointing to a cornice loaded with snow, just waiting for a reason to bury them. Cade got on his radio and communicated their status and she heard something about the potential avalanche.

Just one of many things they'd have to watch for. In the meantime, a helicopter could drop more gear now that the SAR team had made it down. After assessing the climber's injuries, they'd relay their needs to the command center.

Only, Heidi noticed, they weren't dressed like climbers. Coats, sure, but jeans and regular shoes. How could they have hiked all this way this time of year without crampons or snowshoes? Heidi told Cade to request the extra gear and whatever winter hiking wear was available. He arched a brow, the question in his eyes confirming hers, and relayed the information.

What was going on?

* * *

Isaiah caught up with Heidi. She was too stressed for her own good. That could be dangerous. But he knew he was partially to blame for that. Or was he giving himself too much credit?

She'd had a rough time of things the past few months, and Isaiah had pulled away when he'd realized they were growing too close. He couldn't let himself get involved with anyone because of his own mistakes. He wanted to keep the past he ran from hidden. Heidi deserved better than him, and when he'd seen that look in her eyes—one of longing and admiration— a look that he returned too eagerly, he knew he had to withdraw.

And he'd hurt her.

Then came the accident. Heidi had been out for a hike with friends when someone had fallen to their death. Pain zinged through Isaiah. She'd blamed herself, and Isaiah could relate all too well to that feeling. How he wanted to be there for her. To encourage her and get her through it, but he'd already backed away. Let her family be there for her.

And they had been.

Except for when it came to informing Heidi that the man she was seeing, months after Isaiah had made his retreat, was married. Isaiah ended up with that grueling, dirty task. Why him, of all people?

But all that was behind them, and Heidi needed to focus on this rescue. Cade insisted that the only way for her to dig out of the dark place she'd crawled into was to get back into the thick of search and rescue. While that made perfect sense, Isaiah had been worried it was too soon.

He swallowed the sudden knot that arose again as he recalled seeing her dangling on the rope through his night vision goggles moments ago. It was Heidi's decision to be here, and her brother's business to watch out for her. Not Isaiah's, other than as her SAR team member. No. He wasn't in the Warrens' inner circle. Not since he'd severed his emotional connection to Heidi.

And not since Cade had started acting as if something was eating at him. It was unusual for Cade to keep anything from Isaiah. He didn't know what was going on, but he feared his secret was out. Cade was brooding over something and he didn't appear to know how to share it with Isaiah. Now that Isaiah thought about it, Cade had tried to talk to him a few times about whatever was bothering him, but then he'd shut down. What else could it be except that Cade had found out the truth about Isaiah? That was too much to think about on an easy day, so he shook away the thought and concentrated on the rescue.

The moonlight had crept across the sky and into the gap between the two peaks so he tugged his goggles over his helmet and pushed past Heidi, leading the way to the group. They needed to establish that the SAR team was in charge from the very beginning.

As he approached the climbers, two of the men left the circle around the fire and hiked toward him, bundled up in their winter coats, though it was spring. But mountain summits didn't often care. Isaiah squared his shoulders and stood tall as he closed the distance to meet them.

When he reached them, one of the two stepped forward. The leader of this climbing party?

Isaiah thrust his gloved hand out. "Isaiah Callahan, and behind me, Heidi and Cade Warren. We're part of the North Face Mountain Search and Rescue."

"I'm Zach, and this is Jason. Rhea and Liam are by the fire."

Zach was trim enough, though he looked bulky with his coat, but he was about Isaiah's height at five feet eleven inches. Jason was both stockier and taller.

"Good you were able to make a fire." Isaiah

noticed a bruise on Jason's forehead, a cut and smudges across Zach's temple and face. "How are you holding up?"

Jason huffed, and Zach sent him a glare over his shoulder. What was that about?

"Where's the injured party?" Cade asked, coming up behind Isaiah, carrying his pack and ropes.

"We were informed someone had taken a fall." A little breathless, Heidi finally joined them. She handed off the pack holding the medical gear to Isaiah. Though they were each trained to assist in all situations, Isaiah had the most medical experience.

"That was Robbie." Zach gestured to the shadows beyond the fire. "Over there. But he's already gone. No point in worrying about him now."

Was the guy in so much shock he couldn't render any emotion over a fallen friend? The cold words struck Isaiah. He glanced to Cade and Heidi. Did they sense that something was off here, too? He couldn't read them.

Zach led them over to the fire.

The radio squawked and Cade answered, discussing the coordinates and the extra gear the helicopter would drop. He left the group to position himself to receive the goods. Heidi began unpacking, preparing for an overnight stay that would include a winter storm.

Spring didn't mean anything up in the mountains in Alaska's Coast Range.

Letting his gaze skim the fire and the climbers' sorely lacking gear, except for one conspicuous green bag near the fire, he finally spotted the bundle, likely the body, about fifteen or more yards away in the shadows. Isaiah hated hearing they hadn't made it in time to save someone but it happened all too often.

Zach was suddenly at his side again.

"What happened to him?" Isaiah pointed to what he assumed was the body of the injured climber.

"He fell."

"But he was still alive when you called us." They'd gotten here as quickly as they could.

"I don't know, man, you know how these things happen. He fell and his injuries killed him."

Yeah, Isaiah knew. He trudged in the direction of the body, the thrum of a helicopter drawing closer. He glanced over his shoulder and saw Cade's silhouette in the distance as he made his way to gather the gear being dropped.

Something didn't add up. None of the climbers were equipped to climb the summit or traverse the cliff side. How did they get here?

Confusion along with an unwelcome sick feeling that something was definitely wrong crawled over him like a sudden, drastic drop in temperature.

"Where are you going?" Zach followed. "I said he was dead. There's nothing more you can do for him. We need to get out of here tonight. You're wasting time."

Isaiah kept walking. "None of us are getting out tonight."

"What?" The guy jerked Isaiah around.

"A storm's coming. Life Flight is planning to hoist the injured man out of here in the morning, that is, after the storm clears out."

"We don't need to wait."

"The logistics of getting everyone out tonight are a nightmare. In the morning when the storm clears is better. It's safer. And it's the only option."

Isaiah proceeded to the body. He knelt down to examine the man, pulling out his flashlight. Had he died of hypothermia?

Then he found the blood and...a gunshot entry wound. When he was up top, he thought he'd heard a gunshot ring out in the distance behind him, too far to be related to the group in the valley. Had he been wrong about that?

Stiffening, Isaiah slowly pressed his hand inside his parka, covering the weapon in his shoulder holster. He was here to rescue people, not hurt them.

"Don't even think about it." Zach pressed the cold muzzle of a gun against the back of Isaiah's exposed neck.

Closing his eyes, Isaiah sent up a prayer and calculated his next move.

The gun pressed harder, digging into his flesh. "Put your hands up where I can see them and slowly stand up."

Zach backed away from Isaiah as he turned to face the guy, his hands up. Too bad. He could have wrestled the weapon from him.

"He's dead because he'd only slow us down," Zach said. "Are you going to be next?"

TWO

Heidi unpacked the tents and synthetic insulated blankets, tossing them to the wary climbers by the fire. Jason, Liam and then Rhea. The woman, face pale, lips a little blue, wore a dazed expression and shivered. It appeared she might be getting hypothermic. None of that came as a surprise considering the climbers had been waiting for hours for the SAR team to arrive.

Heidi must have let her gaze linger on Rhea too long because the woman blinked and looked up from the fire, regarding Heidi with an odd expression. Heidi hated that Rhea gave her the creeps. She was here to assist Rhea and her climbing buddies, so Heidi didn't like thinking that way about anyone. Yet she almost wished the moon wasn't shining on the woman's face. Soon enough, she'd have her wish as the light in the sky shifted behind the mountains or the storm clouds hid it from view. Unfortunately, she didn't relish working in the dark, either.

Heidi focused her attention back on removing the needed equipment from the various packs. The snow flukes to help secure the tents against the heavy and wet snow, along with the high winds that would come with the expected storm. The small camping stove and fuel they'd mostly use to melt snow for water. Sleeping bags. Now all she needed was some help to get the tents set up.

A blast of icy wind swept over her. It was definitely picking up. She shivered at the thought. Heidi hated to weather a storm like this, but the good thing was they'd gotten here beforehand and these people would have ample protection now. Cade had been right to insist she help. The swell of satisfaction she received when helping others was returning.

"You should wait," Rhea said.

Heidi looked up from the pack—stuff now strewn around. "Wait? Why would I do that? The faster I can get you warmed up the better."

"Because we're hiking out tonight."

The woman wasn't making any sense, didn't know what she was talking about. Yep, her core body temperature was too low. The quicker Heidi got Rhea inside a tent, the better. Heidi glanced at the two men who only stared into the fire. Obviously, they had experience in dealing with Rhea. Heidi would follow their example.

She kept her thoughts to herself and focused on setting up camp. No need to further antagonize Rhea.

Cade had gone off to grab the rest of the supplies the helicopter dropped a few hundred yards from them to keep it safe, and Isaiah went to check on the deceased climber. Not so far away, but they couldn't get back fast enough for her.

"Did you hear me?" Rhea's tone grew belligerent.

What was this all about?

"That was never the plan." Heidi stood tall, facing her. "The plan was that a helicopter would hoist anyone who was injured out in the morning. It's too dangerous tonight."

Cade came from the shadows and tossed more packs and sleeping bags toward Heidi, where they plopped in the snow. Heidi shot him a look.

"What's the problem?" Cade caught his breath, then focused on Rhea. Jason and Liam stood up as if they were answering a challenge.

"No problem," Rhea said. "I told her not to unpack. We're hiking out."

Cade frowned.

Isaiah came into the circle of light, Zach right behind him. Zach shoved Isaiah forward.

What was going on?

Zach held two guns and pointed one at Isaiah and one at Cade. "I'll need your weapons and all communication devices." He glanced over at Heidi. "You, too, sweetheart."

Heidi gulped for air. This couldn't be happening. What would Cade do? She watched him, willing him to hear her pleading.

Don't try to be a hero now, Cade. Please don't.

"I don't have anything on me," Heidi said.

"You're going to have to prove it." Zach waved the gun. "Take off your coats."

"What?" Cade said. "It's too cold out here! We have to stay the night on this mountain."

Zach pressed the gun into Isaiah's temple. "I don't need all three of you."

"Yes, you need us all." Heidi didn't hide the desperation in her plea. "Whatever you're planning, to hike out tonight like Rhea said, you definitely need all three of us. You'll never make it without our help. We are the bare minimum required."

Angling his head, Zach studied her, considering her words.

The way Isaiah slightly shook his head, as though he was ready to die for them right here and now was too much for Heidi. She couldn't allow that. Cade could not get his weapon out in time to do anything for them. Isaiah had to know that.

"Do as he says, Cade." Heidi took off her

own coat and arctic cold swirled around her. She shivered.

Wind rippled over the small fire and almost snuffed it out, but Heidi knew the darkness wouldn't help them.

"You should listen to her," Zach said.

Cade quickly stripped from his jacket, revealing his shoulder holster and the weapon inside. He handed it over to Jason.

"Radios and SAT phones, cell phones, everything."

Cade's expression turned dark and menacing as he handed over everything that would connect him to their brother David, who was monitoring this rescue mission from the command center at the base of the mountain. Adam, Cade and Heidi's other brother, had been called out on a separate search and rescue. The Warren siblings were spread out tonight.

"Is that everything?"

"We came here to help you," Isaiah said. "A storm is approaching, so we don't have time for this. Why are you threatening us, pointing those guns at us?"

"If you don't want our help, we'll just be on our way," Cade said.

"I like to hear that, because that's exactly what's going to happen. We're going to be on our way. All of us. You're going to lead, and we're going to follow you out."

Isaiah looked at the cliff face they'd just scaled. "We're not equipped to help you back up that cliff, not in the dark. Not with a storm closing in. There's a reason we brought supplies to make it through the night and longer, depending on the weather."

"Why did you call us? Why do you need us?" Heidi asked the question, but she thought she already knew the answer.

"The supplies you brought, and we need you to guide us out," Jason said.

Finally, someone besides Zach spoke up. Maybe if they could somehow take him out, the rest of them could be overcome.

"Our small plane crash-landed up there." Jason pointed behind them. "Two people didn't survive, the pilot died. Another guy, too. The rest of us…we made it this far, but knew we needed to call for help or die in the mountains."

But why the guns? Obviously, there was much more to this than they were being told. They were desperate to get out tonight, which was also a risk. So desperate that they would hold a search and rescue team at gunpoint. Why were they in such a hurry? What were they running from?

Fear gripped Heidi at her next thought.

Were they fugitives?

She didn't watch the news enough to know anything.

Heidi wanted to ask, but her brother gave a slight shake of his head. Knowing too much about this group in need of help could be deadly. But sooner or later the SAR team would learn the truth, and Heidi feared that truth, when it came, would cost their lives.

"Look, I don't know why you think you need to hold us at gunpoint. This whole thing is some sort of crazy." Isaiah regretted the words as soon as he said them. "You asked for help and you got it. That's what we're here to do, but you have to trust us. And believe me when I say we can't guide you out of this saddle tonight."

Isaiah's heart battered his insides. He thought he'd already seen enough trouble to last him a lifetime. But he needed to try to talk their way out of this.

Zach didn't appear to like to be challenged, especially in front of his friends. He stepped toward Isaiah, waving his weapons around, his thick gloves raising the threat of him accidentally putting too much pressure on a trigger guard. Isaiah didn't think Zach had the safety locked on either weapon.

An image of a woman covered in blood suffused his mind. He shook the memory. A vise gripped Isaiah's chest. He wanted to grab the guns and stop this insanity.

"Didn't I already warn you that if you slow me down, I'll get rid of you?" Zach aimed both guns at Isaiah, point-blank.

"No!" Heidi screamed.

Zach made a mistake, standing too close. Isaiah could grab him, disarm him, but with Cade and Heidi so near and Jason holding the other weapon, that would gain Isaiah nothing. He couldn't risk someone else's life, but then again, if he didn't take the chance now he was risking all their lives.

To Isaiah's regret, Heidi put herself in the line of fire and pulled on Zach's arm. "Please, don't."

"Get back, Heidi." Isaiah skewered her with his gaze. He didn't need her risking her life for him.

"To get out of these mountains, you need all three of us," she said again.

Zach's gaze slid to Heidi. It was all Isaiah could do to keep from wiping that leer off his face. But he didn't have to worry about it for long. Zach slammed his weapon into the side of Isaiah's head, just under his helmet. He fell back into the snow, dizziness engulfing him.

"Isaiah!" Heidi's scream sounded as if it was coming from the other end of a tunnel.

She appeared by his side. "Isaiah," she whispered. "Talk to me."

He tugged off the helmet and grabbed his head. "These things don't protect against raving lunatics."

What had he expected from Zach, anyway?

"Heidi's right," Cade said to Zach. "We can help you climb out tonight, but it's going to take all three of us."

Ignoring his pounding head, Isaiah focused his vision. He had to stay with it. Heidi scrambled over to the medical kit a few feet away.

"I'm not convinced," Rhea said. She looked at Heidi.

What? That woman expected Zach to do away with Heidi?

Cade's tension was palpable. "In addition to our equipment and expertise, you'll need us to physically assist you down. There are four of you. You need all of us."

Something ran down Isaiah's neck. He pressed his gloved hand against the side of his head where he felt a knot and drew it back. Blood. Zach had given him a gash.

This was an absolute nightmare.

"That settles it, then," Zach said. "Now that we're all in agreement, let's get this stuff put away and get geared up."

Heidi dropped next to Isaiah. She examined

his head and swabbed it, then looked him in the eyes. He wished she wouldn't do that. Give him that look that showed him how much she cared, and yet how much she couldn't care. How much he'd hurt her, on top of everything else that had happened.

"You shouldn't challenge him like that," she whispered. "Just do as they ask. We'll make it out of this. We have to."

She moved to stand, but he grabbed her wrist. "Don't put yourself between me and anyone like that again."

Shaking her head, she tried to stand, but he kept his grip on her. "Do you hear me?"

"You'd do the same for me," she said.

Yes. Yes he would, and more. But he couldn't have her risking her life for the likes of him. He didn't deserve the sacrifice.

Heidi stood and offered her hand. Of course, Isaiah could stand without her help, but he took her hand anyway. Felt the strong, sturdy grip beneath her gloves. Maybe Cade had been right. Heidi needed to get back into climbing and helping people. Search and rescue. Only Isaiah was certain she didn't need it to come at her like this, with crazy people waving guns around.

The moon finally dipped behind the north summit, and the silhouette of thick clouds edged into the sky from the west. Isaiah put his helmet back on.

"Hey!" Zach directed his attention to Isaiah and Heidi. "What are you doing? Let's get the gear packed up and ready to go."

Isaiah growled under his breath. This guy had no idea what he was getting them all into. He bent down to help Heidi pack the tents and stuff the equipment back in the pack. The helicopter had dropped more gear. How were they going to carry all of it down? He watched Cade studying all their supplies, probably wondering the same thing. If they were really going to do this, hike out tonight, at least until the storm prevented them from going farther, there were few items they could do without. Added to that, they had no idea how long Zach and his crew were going to need their assistance.

David monitored their activity from the command center and would want an update soon. Isaiah had no idea what they would tell the man. Did Zach even have a clue about that? And did he have a clue that it might be mid-April but up in these mountains it might as well be the dead of winter? Well, except there was more daylight. The thing was, if they went tromping off into this mountain wilderness and survived, at some point, another team would be sent to search for them when they went missing.

Oh, yeah, someone would look for them.

But the storm could very well prevent that search from happening anytime soon, and with Zach pressing them they could be far from here by then. They might never be found.

How far was Zach planning to push them?

Isaiah finished zipping the last pack, itching to ask Zach exactly that. Just how far were they intending to hike? How long would they need the SAR team's assistance?

How long before Zach killed them?

THREE

Heidi decided to wait until the last possible moment to tug her heavy backpack on. As overfilled as it was, it would weigh her down and tire her out before they made whatever unreasonable destination Zach had in mind. They'd yet to learn where exactly it was he wanted them to guide him other than off this saddle between the summits. All she knew was that leaving tonight was a potentially lethal idea.

Regardless, she couldn't afford to slow them down. By killing the other man in the group, Robbie, Zach had already shown he didn't have patience. Didn't care about others. A radio squawked somewhere. Heidi stiffened. They had to update the command center. That had to be David calling.

Zach approached her. *Why me?* Heidi wanted to be invisible.

Her nerves slid down her back and into the snow at her feet. *Please, God, make me invis-*

ible. She didn't want this man to look at her. To talk to her.

But somehow she knew it was already too late. He'd...*noticed* her. The look in his eyes confirmed it. He tugged her tight and leaned in close, his breath warming her cheek. She could fight him with everything in her and even wound him, but she knew that would only end up hurting Isaiah or her brother in the end. So she stood her ground instead.

Then Zach smirked at Isaiah while he kissed the side of her head. She tried to move away, but Zach held fast. A shudder crawled over her.

Even in the firelight, she saw the murder in Isaiah's dark hazel eyes. She could see Cade's jaw working from where he stood behind Isaiah—the very reaction Zach was going for. This was it then. Zach would use her against them until this was over. She was their weakness. She hoped that his actions meant nothing more than taunting Isaiah and her brother, and had nothing at all to do with an actual attraction to her. *God, please, no.*

Holding her close, Zach pressed the gun against her well-insulated coat. "Say anything wrong, and she pays for it."

He jabbed her rib cage and she winced. With his other hand, he lifted the radio from his pocket and tossed it to Isaiah.

"What do you want me to say, then?" Isaiah's scowl deepened. "What about the body of the guy you shot?"

"Say nothing about him. Tell them everything is going as planned. You're settled in for tonight. But tell them you'll hike out tomorrow. We don't need the helicopter to hoist anyone out, after all. We're all fine here."

Heidi couldn't help but think that was good. David would probably suspect something was wrong but, then again, maybe not. It wasn't as if he could imagine this scenario they'd walked into. He would have no reason not to trust their assessment.

Eyes flashing, Isaiah replied on the radio, relaying all that Zach had demanded. Isaiah's pensive gaze never left Heidi. Something fierce and protective burned there, and it took her breath away. Now she couldn't help but fear for Zach. What would Isaiah do to the man once he got the chance?

She didn't want Isaiah to put himself in harm's way for her, or to do or say something he'd regret later. Finally, Heidi was able to withdraw from Zach, and she noticed Rhea watching her with those crazy eyes.

"Well, then, we're wasting time. Let's gear up and head out." Cade tossed the heavy packs, along with the bags dropped by the helicopter, to each of the climbers, since they apparently didn't have their own gear except for the one green bag.

Jason, Liam and Rhea stared down at the stuff and back up at Zach.

"What's all this?" Rhea asked. "We can't carry this stuff."

Zach shrugged. "We have to make it as far as we can tonight. Do the best you can."

"We'll need as much of that as we can bring." Isaiah tossed headlamps to them.

Heidi almost smiled at that. He always thought of everything. And it was a good thing, too, especially for this unexpected situation because these people wouldn't be able to see their way down. Maybe if the SAR team could show them what exactly they faced rappelling, Zach would change his mind. But he appeared to be a man on a mission and nothing would stop him.

The big question of the day: What was driving him?

This was insane. She didn't want to be anywhere nearby if one of them fell or got hurt. She couldn't go through that again. She had no idea what kind of shape this motley crew of criminals was in, but she'd guess they had no clue what they were in for.

Cade folded up the map he'd been looking at

and tucked it in his coat. He started off, heading southwest. "Let's go, then."

Unmoving, Zach cocked his head.

"Wait," Isaiah said. "Why that way?"

Are you kidding me? She wished he'd stop talking. Zach looked irritated anytime Isaiah said anything, making her more scared that he would be the first of them to go. Something inside whimpered at the thought. But…how could this end any other way?

"Isaiah," she said, hoping she didn't have an audience. Everyone seemed preoccupied with their gear.

When he gazed at her, she willed him to understand, read her thoughts. *Don't stir up more trouble for us. Just follow Cade.*

But she knew Isaiah and Cade hadn't been getting along the past few weeks, and that would probably play into this whole mess. She hoped she wasn't the cause of the rift between them.

Isaiah directed his next words to Cade. "We need to talk about the best way down. If we choose the wrong way, we could all die."

Isaiah knew what Heidi wanted. She wanted him to follow her brother, like always, but maybe neither one of them was thinking right. Maybe Isaiah was the only one capable of thinking this through.

Cade got in Isaiah's face. He sure wished he could use this to his advantage like he'd seen in the movies. He and Cade distract the bad guys and then punch them. Take them out. But no. That wasn't going to happen tonight.

Fury rippled in Cade's overstressed face. "We hike out through Rush Gulley. It's the only way."

"Not with the storm coming. We'll be too exposed and get the brunt of it on that side of the mountains. Our whole purpose in bringing this gear is to make it through the night. Protect them from the storm. The deadly temps."

Cade worked his jaw and looked away, breathing hard, pondering Isaiah's words.

Then Zach was in the middle, playing with his gun again. "Do I need to kill one of you so we don't have to waste time arguing on the best way out? We hike out the safest and fastest way to the ice field."

"What?" So there it was. Zach's destination. "Why the ice field?"

"Because that's my only ride out of this frozen world. I have four days to get there."

"We'll never make it," Cade said. "That's too far."

"It's only thirty miles. We're that close. So we take shortcuts if we have to. Go over the mountains instead of around them. You can do it. You're mountain climbers." Zach grinned.

As if that would appease or charm them into agreeing. Isaiah wanted to punch him. They didn't have all the gear they'd need for such a trek. Or the food or supplies. It was a death wish at best.

In this weather and terrain, they'd be fortunate to make five or six miles a day, tops, and that wasn't counting the added burden of inexperienced climbers. Isaiah wanted to inform him there was no possible way, but he'd already done enough damage.

"Safest and fastest don't go together," he said.

The temperature dropped as the storm pushed arctic air deeper into the mountains. Isaiah sometimes wondered how it could get colder. They needed to keep moving or they'd get hypothermic right here. They needed to get the blood pumping. Sure, he wanted to take Zach down, but first and foremost, he was part of a search and rescue team, and he'd see this through. He'd get these people out and to safety, and then let the authorities deal with them. He didn't want to hurt them.

Unless he had to. He would do whatever was necessary to protect Cade and Heidi. His heart staggered at the thought of harm coming to her.

Hands at his hips, he looked at the ground, waiting for Cade to say something. He didn't want to get into it with him, but he'd needed to question Cade on his decision. He doubted any of them were thinking as clearly as they could under the circumstances.

"Isaiah's right," Cade said. "The north face will be tough going down. But it's the quickest way to your destination, so you should be glad about that. You'll have to stick very close to us, but I figure we have an hour, maybe two before we have to set up the tents to weather the storm."

"No. We keep going," Zach said.

"We won't make it if we don't stop. The storm will be a blizzard. A whiteout. Do you get that? We won't be able to see where we're going, even with night goggles and headlamps. We couldn't even if we were in broad daylight. This terrain is deadly all by itself. Be realistic, man."

Still looking at his boots sunk in the snow, Isaiah shook his head, mostly to himself. There was no good way out of here in the dark during a storm. But if he put himself in Zach's head, maybe he could imagine why the guy was so desperate.

"I get it," he said. "You want us to be gone by morning, so if the storm clears out, we'll be untraceable."

Zach nodded to Isaiah, respect in his eyes. Isaiah couldn't say he returned the sentiment.

"So tell me." He was going to do this thing.

Ask the forbidden question that he knew Cade and Heidi wanted the answer to, too. But they were afraid to know the truth. The way Isaiah figured it, their lives were already forfeit. Might as well know the whole of it. "What or who are you running from? What did you do?"

The guy's eyes narrowed.

"Come on, man. We're risking our lives for you out here. Tell us what this is all about."

"Isaiah, no. We don't need to know what's going on." Cade glared at Isaiah, then directed his words to Zach and the others. "It's none of our business. All we care about is getting you out of here and to safety, and we want to be left to make our own way. Let's agree on that."

Cade was right, and Isaiah had proven himself a bigger idiot than he thought possible.

Jason stepped up next to Zach, his headlamp blinding them.

"Armored-car robbery," he said. "That's what."

Cade's form deflated as he blew out a big breath. The look of pained disappointment he gave Isaiah hit him in the gut. He'd pushed things too far, he saw that now. Cade was right. They didn't want to know what this was about. Isaiah had just sealed their fates.

"We escaped," Jason continued. "Made it out. Nobody had a clue where to look. Then we hit a snag in Zach's big plans when our plane crashed. You want to know how much money?"

Jason opened his mouth and sucked in a breath, but Zach punched him in the face.

Grabbing his nose, Jason howled and cursed Zach. "What'd you do that for?"

With a single look, Zach silenced him. Too bad that couldn't have worked to begin with, before the punch to the face.

"Now if we're done with the small talk, lead on." Zach gestured ahead of him.

The wind picked up and the snow clouds slowly crept across the sky. Once the clouds blanketed the region and hid the moon, this clan would depend completely on the goggles and headlamps. And once the storm hit, their feeble lighting would be of little help.

Before he turned to lead the way, Cade gave Isaiah one long shake of his head. Isaiah hoped Cade could see the regret in his eyes, but he was sure it wouldn't matter. This wasn't the first time Cade had given him that disappointed look lately, but at least this time Isaiah knew the reason for it. Now wasn't the time to try to figure out what had been bothering his friend, especially since he likely already knew the answer to that. He tried to shove the unwelcome thoughts out of the way.

They would have to work together as a team

in a way they never had before. This would require all their energy and focus and trust.

Trust. Why had this particular search and rescue scenario hit them when the trust between the three of them was at an all-time low?

Let it go, man. You don't have time to worry about that now.

Carrying the heavy packs and gear, everything they'd need to survive, the group trudged behind Cade as he led the way off the saddle, careful to stay out of the path of the avalanche that could spill from the cornice above at any moment.

Zach hiked next to Isaiah, pulling up the back, and pointing his gun at Isaiah for fun. "Don't forget that I have guns. Will kill."

"Well, Zach, I'm intimidated by you, sure," Isaiah said. This guy felt big and strong with the weapons he didn't handle all that well. "But facing off with nature in this part of the world scares me more. If you're not scared yet, you will be."

FOUR

Heidi struggled to keep up with Cade. With his big strides, he covered the ground quickly, even in the snow-covered saddle. None of the SAR team members had removed their crampons yet, and they hadn't tasked the climbers to wear them or snowshoes until required. The snow wasn't loose enough that they sank into it here, but the terrain indicated that they were approaching a sharp drop.

That was only one problem they would eventually face. Added to that, they'd have to be sure this group knew how to use an ice ax for self-rescue, or a technical ice ax if required. *Argh.* Did they even have all the equipment they would need? She doubted it. Heidi's breathing hitched. She wanted to pull her hair out. This wasn't going to work.

Straight ahead, on the other side of the peak across from them, she could see the silhouette of Devil's Paw, the highest point on the

Juneau Icefield, which marked the border between southeast Alaska and British Columbia. And just below that, though she couldn't see it, Michael's Sword thrust upward from the ice field, like its namesake blade.

Even if Heidi couldn't see much through the night vision goggles, she knew they were about to face their first taste of terror. Cade knew that, too, and likely feared how much worse it would be if they didn't make good time and find a place to hunker down in their tents. All because they had to please the madman who'd called them in to rescue him.

Clouds crept forward, the edges reminding her of pointed fingers, creeping toward the moon. With the summit looming above them to the north, Heidi wished she had her camera to capture this amazing image. But even if she did, she couldn't fathom stopping to enjoy her hobby.

Once the moon finally died a silent death behind the sword-clouds, Heidi would lose sight of Cade without her night vision goggles. Zach's gang had been instructed to wait to use their headlamps until absolutely necessary to save the batteries.

Heidi felt as if she was in a space suit again, her clothing thick, her movements slow—only she'd never wanted to be an astronaut. Never wanted to go to the moon. This might be exactly how it felt to be there, except, of course, her steps would cause her to bounce instead of sink.

Snow swirled as the wind picked up. Oh, no. Were they walking right into the screaming wind tunnel again? Or worse, was the storm on them already? She thought her space suit might be running out of oxygen. Though her breaths came fast and hard, dragging in the frigid air, she still couldn't get enough of it.

Oh, Lord. Not here. Not now.

Breathe in, breathe out. Her lungs screamed. An iceberg of pressure weighed on her chest. And her head.

Heidi stopped and ripped off the helmet and goggles, grabbing her head. Would it explode?

Cade had always been there for her, but no—he trudged ahead as if he was the only one who mattered. Isaiah's face filled her vision. He'd removed his goggles and helmet, revealing his thick brown hat-hair, the moonlight caressing enough of his face that she could see the undeniable concern in his eyes.

He gripped her upper arms. "Heidi, what's wrong?"

"I—" she gasped for breath. "I—"

"Slowly." Isaiah pressed his gloved hands to the sides of her head. "You have to breathe slowly."

How did he know? Heidi focused on his

gaze and the emotions she couldn't read swirling there. She had the sense that he was barely holding back a torrent of them. She calmed a little, her breathing easing, but the reason for her panic hadn't dissipated. Everyone stood around her, watching her as if she was some kind of mental case. What if Zach decided to kill her because of it?

"Are we really going to do this?" she asked. "Are we really going to hike down with inexperienced climbers in the dark and—"

"Shh." He pressed a finger against her lip, and it was surprisingly warm. When had he removed his gloves? "This is a search and rescue mission just like any other. You've trained for this, you can do it."

Zach pulled Isaiah away from Heidi. She hated him for it. *Isaiah, whatever happened to us?*

Oh, no, here it comes. He's going to kill me now. She and Isaiah never even had their chance, or rather, a second chance.

"You know I like you, sweetheart, but if you're not careful you might outlive your usefulness. Let's get moving."

Heidi saw Cade ahead of them watching her, but then he turned around and hiked forward at breakneck speed. Isaiah gave her a reassuring nod and tugged his helmet and goggles back

on. She followed his example and hiked next
to him, drawing strength and confidence from
him. She had strength, too. She just had to dig
down deep and find where it had hidden and
pull it out. *This is a search and rescue mission just like any other.* She could do this. And
as for anything else, like escaping? As long as
Zach, Jason and Liam, and possibly Rhea, carried weapons, there wasn't much else they could
do except follow orders.

Wait and pray.

A new team would be sent to search for them
at some point when they didn't show up. But
Heidi dreaded how long that would take. SAR
volunteers were already stretched thin due to
two ongoing rescue operations before Cade,
Heidi and Isaiah had been delivered to the drop
point near the summit.

How long before David began to worry?
How long before they could even send a team
to search for them? And if they did, she'd bet
David and Adam would both be on that team.
But the farther they trekked into the deep mountain wilderness, the less chance they had of
being found, especially with a man like Zach,
who would do everything within his power to
keep their whereabouts hidden.

No. She couldn't count on being rescued.
They were on their own.

No one knew they'd sent the search and rescue team to face a killer. Or killers. No one knew they were headed to the ice field. Making it there in this weather? That was another story altogether.

Cade stopped and held up his hand, signaling for the rest of them to stop.

Heidi closed the distance to stand just behind him. She sucked in a breath. Rush Gulley, Cade's initial suggestion, would have been so much easier than this jagged, angular descent into the lower ridge on this side of the mountain. She wouldn't want to do this on a good day, much less a stormy night. What would Zach's cronies say when they saw this, though their view would be limited?

"Looks like I'm up," she said. She had more experience in multipitch technical climbing, though both Isaiah and Cade could hold their own.

"Wrong. I'll go down first, make sure there's no loose rocks or hazards. And I'll untie them once they're lowered to the bottom. That's all we're doing here, lowering them down."

Heidi wanted to argue, but giving him a spiel about working as a team right now would be pure bad timing. Cade had always been the team leader, and that's just the way it was, so she held her tongue.

He shook his head. "I don't like this. Why did I listen to Isaiah?"

"He was right, that's why." She steadied her breathing, reining in the panic that threatened beneath the surface again. "We're a team, Cade, so we have to start acting like one. Granted, this is the worst possible scenario, but we pass this test tonight, and we can't face anything worse."

Except maybe a bullet to the head.

There. She got in her spiel after all, and reassurance for the both of them, too.

"Whatever we do has to be quick, or we're going to get caught in the jaws of something driving, cold and wet. I don't like keeping these people, no matter their crime, out in the elements any longer than necessary."

Isaiah stepped next to them. "Let's get busy then. We can rig a seat harness for this, and anything else we face. No point in risking their lives by letting them attempt to climb."

Even Zach looked a little daunted as he peered into what, for him, with only a headlamp, would be a bottomless abyss. "What's the plan?"

"You're forcing us to go on a suicide mission, that's the plan," Heidi said. "We need to set up the tents and wait out the storm. Not climb down some insane multipitch terrain at night."

It was worth a try anyway.

Isaiah dumped his pack and began setting up everything to lower them down.

A creepy grin slid onto Zach's face. "But here you are, preparing to do exactly that. You're turning out to be useful, after all. I'm glad, because I wasn't ready to leave you behind. Not yet."

Frowning, Isaiah motioned for Heidi to join him and help. She was grateful for the excuse to get out from under Zach's gaze. But his words clung to her just the same. Isaiah set up an anchor around a rock, and Heidi clipped a carabiner—a small oval ring used as a connector—to hold the belay device, which was used to create friction on the rope, in place for lowering the climbers.

"So, um, what should we do to get ready?" Jason asked. "We don't have climbing gear."

Very perceptive.

"Pray. That's what you should do." Isaiah worked with the tubular webbing they always carried to create the right seat harness.

Depending on the situation and injuries, they could create whatever kind of harness they needed for the person or persons they rescued.

"That is," Isaiah said, looking up from his task, "if you consider yourself a praying man, Jason. We need a lot of prayer if we're going to live through the night."

* * *

Two hours later, Isaiah knew someone had been praying.

Shivering at the bottom of another ridge cutting between the mountains—which kept them in the upper elevations—they quickly assembled the three tents, all geared with the required flies, sealed seams and enough extra snow flukes to withstand the approaching blizzard. Then supplies of water and food were dispersed among each shelter. They'd only brought one cooking stove with fuel, though.

Regardless of their predicament, relief coursed through Isaiah that they'd been successful in lowering their charges and setting up a camp, all in the middle of a frozen night. All as the storm closed in on them. Still, he wasn't sure he could ever shake Rhea's shrieks as they lowered her.

Zach had finally agreed to stop but only after Rhea's terrifying experience down the terrain had left her crying and pitching a fit. She demanded they stop and wait until daylight. Isaiah could see that she would freeze to death if they kept going, as it was. Inside the tent, she could get warm in a sleeping bag and then get into the better winter wear they'd brought with them.

Isaiah finished building a snow wall around the last tent to protect it from the gale-force winds, and couldn't wait to climb in and warm up. Rest his weary bones and mind. Except, depending on how fast the snow accumulated, he'd have go back outside to dig them out at regular intervals. Too much snow could collapse the tent.

Zach approached and shoved him with his foot, his headlamp flickering. "One of you sleeps with each of us in a tent. Rhea and Heidi are together."

Isaiah stood to face the man. "There's nowhere for us to run."

"Get in." Zach held his weapon.

Did Zach know how to clean the snow and weather out of the bore so it wouldn't malfunction? Just before Isaiah climbed into the tent, he saw Cade and Heidi, and shared a look of regret with each of them.

Isaiah had a feeling he knew what they were both thinking. Once they got Zach and his men and woman to safety, they would likely be killed. They knew more than they should know about the armored-car robbers and killers. Knew their faces and their names. He squatted and crawled into the tent. What a weird twist of fate, to save people knowing they would kill you when you finally delivered them to safety. Isaiah crawled over to the sleeping bag to the right, making it his own. He dropped down and didn't bother taking off his coat. Not warm enough inside yet.

At least tonight he would be warm and dry, despite the nefarious company.

Their supplies were limited because they hadn't expected they would be hiking through the frozen Alaska wilderness. They were all too exhausted tonight to use the small camping stove they'd brought to warm up their water. But if they were in this very long, they'd need to conserve the fuel to melt snow. For now, keeping warm was a matter of bundling up in the sleeping bags and combined body heat to warm up the inside of the tent.

Zach and Liam crawled inside, too, looking as haggard as Isaiah felt. He guessed Jason was with Cade and he knew Rhea was with Heidi. Why did they have to be separated in the first place? He wasn't sure he could sleep for worrying that he would be killed in the night, or that Cade or Heidi would face the same fate.

He pinched the bridge of his nose and squeezed his eyes shut. *God, help us.*

"Praying again?" Zach asked.

Isaiah didn't have the energy for this. "You might try it sometime."

Zach and Liam laughed, though Isaiah consoled himself with the fact it was tired and weak.

"I'm starving. What have we got to eat?" Liam dug through the pack inside the tent.

"MREs and energy bars. I'd recommend the energy bar. Quick and simple." Isaiah was too bushed to eat one. He'd get one in the morning.

"They might try to contact us again, you know. So be ready to toss me the radio." Isaiah prepared to slip into the sleeping bag and prayed he could actually sleep. This was going to be a long night. A long, hard journey to the ice field.

"Don't give me orders." Zach held up a rope, then proceeded to tie Isaiah's wrists. "I won't bother tying your ankles. You're not going any-where."

Now it was Isaiah's turn to laugh, and his wasn't so feeble. "Now that I'm all tied up, you get to go outside and scrape the snow off before it gets too heavy or buries us alive in the tent."

Liam stiffened. He looked to Zach for an-swers. When he got none, he studied Isaiah. "How often do we have to do that?"

Isaiah shrugged. "Depends on the storm. I'd say every hour for starters. Then if it snows hard enough, maybe every fifteen minutes."

"How will we know?"

"You'll know." Isaiah lay back down on the sleeping bag, grateful for small things. He wouldn't have to dig them out tonight. He could actually sleep, maybe, and trust God to make it peaceful.

"I say when. Remember, you're not in charge. I am."

A raging retort surged to Isaiah's lips, and he tried holding himself in check but failed. "Really? We just saved your lives tonight. And we delivered you down to this ridge under impossible circumstances. You couldn't have done that on your own."

"Whatever."

Isaiah sat up, adrenaline coursing through him once again. He needed to say the words. Get them out. He pointed a finger at Zach, holding up both tied hands. "That was the hardest thing I've ever done, *we've* ever done, as a team. Don't expect us to do anything like that again. You're fortunate that we all survived. But don't push it."

"You guys are as good as it gets, there's no doubt there. I know what to expect from you now. How hard I can push."

Isaiah believed that God had protected them. Answered their prayers. But as to how hard Zach could push them? Isaiah didn't bother answering. Zach wouldn't listen anyway. He had nothing to lose by pushing them.

Liam turned the flashlight off. They lay in the darkness, the storm beginning to rage around them. Isaiah couldn't stand to think about what tomorrow would bring, and hoped he would drift quickly to sleep, but escape plans exploded in his head.

If they'd retained their weapons, they could have won the day. Maybe. But they'd been caught off guard.

And…Heidi.

A pang stabbed through him. Why did she have to be the one to come? Isaiah couldn't stand that it was Heidi with them. Not on this mission. But he'd better not say that to Heidi. Still, she had to see that Zach appeared intent on using her against Isaiah and Cade.

Isaiah thought back to the good times they'd shared since he'd met her. He'd run from Montana to hide in Mountain Cove, Alaska. Even changed his name to start a new life.

He'd been struck by her soft, kind and huge brown eyes and that dark mahogany mane of hers. But the most beautiful part of her was on the inside. What man wouldn't be attracted to her? He'd done well enough, keeping his distance. They worked together for one thing. Or used to before he'd changed his schedule around. But he'd been able to keep his relationship with her as an easy friendship, that is, until that day not quite a year ago.

The sunset had dazzled them with the most

amazing hues of orange and pink as they stood looking out over the channel, waiting for Cade and Leah to return from another trip to Seattle. Isaiah's gaze had veered from the sunset to Heidi, and he'd made the mistake of letting himself take her in for a little too long. When she looked at him—something happened between them. Something and yet nothing at all. He couldn't put words to it. But they'd connected. He'd felt it. She'd felt it. He *knew* she had. Maybe it had been building for a long time.

He also knew that he'd hurt her by backing away.

But what else could he do? He couldn't let himself get close to anyone like that. Not after everything he'd been involved in. He was almost thankful the wind howled outside the tent as it drowned out his sullen thoughts. On the other hand, it brought him back to their deadly predicament.

FIVE

Heidi opened her eyes. Something had jarred her awake.

She couldn't see her hand in front of her face. The storm wailed outside. What could she have heard over the din? Was Rhea still asleep, or moving around in the tent? Maybe she planned to smother Heidi in her sleep.

Or was it one of the guys scraping the snow off their tent? Liam had informed them earlier that he and Jason had been tasked with the job.

Wary, she shifted inside the insulated sleeping bag, grateful for the smallest of comforts, but concerned about sleeping in the tent with Rhea. Thank goodness they had both collapsed with exhaustion, or at least Heidi thought Rhea had conked out first. The woman had creeped Heidi out from the beginning of this ordeal, and she hadn't relished the idea of sharing tent space with her, but better Rhea than one of the others in Zach's mangy troop.

Rhea was a weird person, and had to be more than a little disturbed to be with a guy like Zach. To admire him. Heidi sensed Rhea's pure and lethal hatred toward her because of Zach's unwarranted attention. Couldn't the woman see that Zach was simply using Heidi against Cade and Isaiah?

Except that wasn't completely true, either. There was something about Heidi that Zach liked. A girl just knew these things. A chill scuttled over her, even though the inside of the tent was relatively warm.

Why had she let her mind take her down this path? She needed sleep, and thinking about the crazy people who could kill them at some point didn't help. They had to get out of this.

Heidi repositioned herself and sighed.

"What's with all the racket over there?" Rhea asked.

"I'm not doing anything. It's the storm."

"I hear you sighing and huffing and puffing. Every time you move in that sleeping bag, I hear it."

Maybe Heidi had been the one to make the noise and had woken herself up. "I'm sorry."

"I don't know why I had to be in here with you instead of with Zach."

"Do you love him, Rhea?" Now, why had

Heidi asked the woman such a question? Why *else* would she be with a man like that?

"Why? You think you can have him? Well, he's mine. All mine."

"That's not why I asked. I can't sleep. I'm just trying to figure out why this is happening to me, Cade and Isaiah. I can't figure out why you would love a criminal." Or maybe Rhea had been in on the heist. Heidi had better keep her mouth shut. Rhea snorted. "Zach is brilliant. He needed money to get started, that's all. Wealthy people aren't going to miss two million dollars."

Two million dollars? Heidi held her breath. Did Rhea realize she'd just shared that information? Zach wouldn't be happy to hear that, but Heidi wouldn't be the one to tell him so it probably didn't matter that she knew.

But…two million dollars. *Oh, God in heaven, help us out of this.*

"Now that I told you about the money, don't think you can steal Zach away from me. I'd kill you first."

Heidi frowned. What kind of person thought like that? Had Rhea been institutionalized at some point? She sounded like some sort of female Praetorian Guard, an elite bodyguard for her emperor, Zach, whom she worshipped. Besides looking and acting crazy, she sounded crazy, which meant Heidi was in even more danger. They all were.

"You don't have to worry about me. I have no interest in Zach. I've learned the hard way that people can't be trusted when it comes to relationships. I don't want to love anyone."

First, Isaiah had distanced himself. Then Lon... Pain knifed through her heart—he'd been a married man, for crying out loud. She could never get over the fact that she'd been romantic with a married man. How his wife must feel about her. She turned in the sleeping bag, not caring if she made Rhea mad. A hot tear slid down the side of her face and right over the bridge of her nose. It dropped to the bedding below. Then she'd learned that her own father, whom she'd loved and adored and admired, had cheated on her mother.

She swiped at the tear then thrust her hands back in the bag.

Rhea didn't say anything to Heidi's comment about relationships, so she added, "Be careful, Rhea. Zach could break your heart."

Heidi should be more concerned about living through this than whether or not Zach would break Rhea's heart, which he would undoubtedly do. She didn't want to trust or love again or feel that pain, but every time she looked at

Isaiah, she wished she could feel a different way. Wished he hadn't hurt her.

What had happened between them?

Earlier tonight, he'd been right there, helping her through her panic as if he'd never left her side—physically or emotionally.

"You're a liar," Rhea said.

"What have I lied about?"

"There is someone you want to love."

Heidi held her breath. What had she done or said to give Rhea that impression? "You're wrong."

Rhea's laugh was deep and raspy, a sick, mocking sound. Where had Zach found her? Heidi's pulse ratcheted up, although it was already near racing. Would Rhea tell Zach, causing him to use Isaiah or Cade—both of whom meant everything—against her?

Wait. Isaiah meant everything? "I don't love anyone. And I don't want anyone. But I'll make you a deal."

"What's that?"

"Remember when Zach punched Jason in the nose because he almost told us how much money you stole?"

Rhea was silent, but Heidi knew she remembered. They all did.

"Zach doesn't want anyone to know how much, but you just told me that he stole two million dollars. That can be our little secret. So I'll keep your secret, if you'll keep mine. Do we have a deal?"

"Yes." Rhea's voice cracked. Was the woman that scared? "Zach will kill me if he finds out."

Tension crept back into Heidi's body. She wouldn't fall back asleep now. Heidi had some power over Rhea, but she could never use it because then Rhea could tell Heidi's secret. Not that she'd admitted to anything.

But the images of what Zach could do tormented her like the howling wind outside.

The radio squawked. Funny the places those things would pick up, and then sometimes when you needed them the most, they failed. But that's why the SAR teams carried a couple of different kinds as well as a SAT phone. Isaiah also took his cell on rescues, which would give off a ping if kept on. Zach had commandeered all their communications equipment except, well, the avalanche beacons, but those weren't exactly communication devices unless you were buried in the snow. Isaiah had turned on his beacon to transmit, anyway, but where they were, nobody was near enough to pick up that signal. No one even knew to look.

Snuggled inside the sleeping bag with his hands tied, he bolted up, oriented himself to his surroundings and spotted the radio on the floor next to Zach's sleeping bag. Didn't the guy hear that? Admittedly, the noise had to burrow into Isaiah's head to get him to wake up.

David was calling to check on his team. Isaiah figured it might be better if he didn't answer, let them start worrying sooner, except there was no getting them out of this place with the inclement weather and gale-force winds still screaming outside. At least morning had broken. That was an advantage they hadn't had last night, and yet somehow they had survived.

He'd give God the credit.

David sounded agitated. Maybe…maybe Isaiah could somehow let David in on what was happening. Give him a clue, if nothing else, but only if Zach and Liam slept through this.

Isaiah worked his way free of the bag and scrambled over to pick up the radio with his hands tied. "I'm here, David!"

The next thing he knew, Zach sprang from where he slept and pressed his gun against Isaiah's temple. Tension corded around his throat and tightened. He couldn't speak.

"Isaiah! Finally. I thought you ran into trouble."

He found his voice. "You could say that."

Zach shoved Isaiah's head with the gun. A clear warning.

Isaiah quickly added, "We're still weathering the storm. But you can be sure we're going to deliver the climbers down the mountain into the right hands."

He wasn't sure why he added those last words, but he had every intention of doing just that. However that played out. Whatever Zach thought he would pull off here, wasn't going to happen if Isaiah—and he knew Cade and Heidi would be with him on this—had anything to do with it. He'd think of something before this was all over. Something before Zach killed them.

"How's Adam? Did his team make it back yet?" Isaiah knew that Cade and Heidi would want to know about their younger brother.

"Yeah. Last night. Found a little boy who'd gotten lost hiking with his parents."

"That's good to hear." At least someone had found success.

"I need your updates more frequently."

"Sure, every hour?"

Zach snatched the radio from him. "If you do that again, you can say goodbye to the woman."

When Zach put the radio to Isaiah's mouth, his eyes narrowed.

"I'll try," Isaiah said, "but we're getting buried here and we're busy."

Zach leaned in and whispered, "Heidi."

Isaiah closed his eyes at his next words.

"Don't worry about us. You know we'll be fine. I'll contact you with coordinates for an extraction point. We'll hike as far as we can first. Could be tomorrow maybe."

"Is Cade around? Why doesn't he answer his radio?"

What? Didn't David trust Isaiah? But then Cade was his brother. Isaiah should understand that. "He's outside, brushing snow off. Heidi's in another tent."

"Okay, then. You guys take care."

"Tell him over and out." Zach nudged him with the gun again.

Huh? They never used that. But Isaiah could use it now. The radio at his mouth, he said, "Over and out."

Would David hear that for what it was? Would he pick up on the clue that Zach had forced Isaiah to drop?

The radio conversation over, Zach shoved Isaiah to the ground. He couldn't stop the fall with his wrists tied. "You ever try that again and I won't kill you. I'll hurt you and leave you to die a slow death."

"The radio had been squawking for a while, and you guys snored through it. Next time I'll just let the command center wonder what happened to us. Let them think we need our own rescue team, if you prefer."

Zach studied Isaiah, considering his words and that outcome. The tent shuddered, fierce wind breaking through the snow wall.

He growled. "It's April, for crying out loud. Why is this happening?"

"This mountain range has some of the roughest weather in the world. That's why. Your plane had the great misfortune of crash-landing here." Isaiah wanted to know where they'd been heading. Had they come from the Alaska mainland running from an armored-car robbery there? Or were they leaving the Lower 48 on their way to Alaska or Canada? But he wouldn't make the same mistake he'd made before and ask.

"Let's pack up. We have to get going."

"No. We have to wait out the storm."

"There's no time. I have four days, now three, to get where I need to be for my ride out of here."

"If you wanted to go on a suicide mission, why did you call for our help? Huh? Tell me that." Isaiah didn't bother to rein in his temper. "You called us to help you out of here. Hear those winds out there? It's a whiteout. We hike out there now and we won't be able to see a thing. It'll be worse than last night. At least we had the night vision goggles then."

"Maybe he's right, Zach." Liam rubbed his tired eyes like a three-year-old. "Let's at least wait until there's a break in the storm. We could make some headway then."

"I need to talk to the others on my team," Isaiah said. "Figure out the quickest and safest way to the ice field. Believe me, I want this to be over with as soon as possible. Just like you." Isaiah held out his hands. "Mind untying me now?"

Zach nodded to Liam. "Untie him, then go get the other one."

Liam's eyes widened. "You want me to go out there?"

"If you don't want me to leave you behind when we leave, then yes, go and get him."

Backing down, Liam shook his head. Zach trained his weapon on Isaiah as if he expected Isaiah to try something as soon as his hands were free. And when Liam left, he just might. But then he thought of Cade and of Heidi.

Liam grabbed his coat and put on his gloves. The tent was small, but at least it was warm.

Isaiah rubbed his hands and wrists. "I'm going to need Heidi, too. She's part of the team."

"It'll get too crowded in here." Zach shifted on his sleeping bag as if he was already feeling claustrophobic.

"Well, I'm sorry about that, but I need her help to plan our next move." He needed her to be here with him. Needed to know she was all right after a night with Rhea, although he knew that Heidi could win that battle, if it came to that, hands down.

"All right." Zach glared at Liam.

The guy unzipped the tent and cold and snow rushed inside. Liam hesitated and Zach kicked him the rest of the way out. There was a chance, though slight, that Liam would get lost altogether and wander into the blizzard, missing the tent. "The next tent over is to your left, Liam," Isaiah shouted.

He wasn't sure Liam heard him. He should be the one to go out there. "I don't know if Liam has it in him to find the other tents in this storm."

Zach scrunched up his face. "He's not an idiot. He was out moving snow off the tents half the night. I think he'll be fine."

"Have you been out in that yet? Do you even know what you're talking about?"

The man shrugged.

Isaiah sent up a prayer.

"You praying again?"

"Yep. Praying that Liam doesn't lose his way."

Zach's face paled. "How could he? The tents are right there."

"You've never been in a blizzard like this. It's called a whiteout for a reason. You can't see where the sky meets the ground. You can't see where you're going. You can even get vertigo."

"That sounds like a bunch of bologne to me."

Was that the answer? Should they just let Zach have his way and try to lead him and his crew out during the whiteout? No. Then they would all be at risk.

A few minutes passed. "Let's pull out the food, get it ready for the others."

Isaiah busied himself starting up the small camping stove. He opened the vents in the tent.

"What's taking him so long?" Zach raked his hand through his hair. "How hard could it be?"

"You should have been the one to go." Isaiah decided he took a little too much pleasure in taunting this guy. "I can go check on them if you want."

"No. You stay right here."

"Okay, then we're both left to wonder if he even made it." Planting the seed of fear in Zach had worked out better than Isaiah thought.

Zach was suddenly in Isaiah's face, pressing the muzzle of his gun under his chin. "You'd love that, wouldn't you? One down, three to go."

Should he wrestle with Zach? Take the gun from him? It was now or never. Squeezing his eyes shut, he reined in the images of taking the gun from Zach. What would that gain him?

Jason still had a weapon trained on Cade. He wasn't sure if Rhea had one, as well.

All he knew was that this wasn't the right moment.

Someone unzipped the tent and stepped inside.

Heidi.

Isaiah's heart jumped.

Cade followed.

Isaiah had made the right decision—wrestling with the weapon could have set it off and killed her or Cade.

Liam tried to come inside, too.

"Go with Jason," Zach said. "There's not enough room here."

Heidi sent Isaiah a soft smile, the strain of a restless night in her face. She crawled over next to him, took off her gloves and shrugged out of her coat. "It's warm in here. How are you holding up?"

"Good."

She slid her hand over his and squeezed.

Isaiah tried to ignore what her touch did to his heart. He pulled his hand away.

God, I have to get her out of here.

Maybe if he could save her—and Cade, too— then Isaiah could redeem himself. Although he knew that wasn't true. Only Christ was the true Redeemer. But maybe if he could right this wrong, it would be something. Although he hadn't been arrested or convicted, hadn't killed anyone, he knew in some roundabout way, he'd played a role in that murder.

SIX

Bundled in her winter gear, Heidi exited the tent.

They'd stared at the maps long enough.

Conserving what water they had, Heidi had used the camping stove to melt snow to drink, and portioned out the energy bars. When the wind had died down, the quiet drew them outside to assess the damage.

Cade, Isaiah and Zach stood next to the snow wall. The tents were nearly buried again, even though the men had taken turns scraping off the snow. Liam, Jason and Rhea were still eating their energy bars, their gazes drawn to the exquisite splendor surrounding them—a pristine but deadly beauty that had threatened their lives.

Indescribable.

The clouds thinned enough that the sun tried to break through. Heidi wanted to celebrate, but she knew the lull in the storm might not last.

"Let's get going." Zach started taking down the tent closest to him.

Everyone followed his lead, that is, everyone except Isaiah.

"I don't think this is the end of the storm." Isaiah followed Zach. "We could get stuck out there, in the thick of it, and this time we could all die."

Zach turned on him. "Do your job, man. Pack up the camp and let's move."

Unfortunately, Heidi had made the mistake of watching the exchange, and caught Zach's attention. Isaiah must have noticed, too, because he looked ready to take Zach down. At some point, they should definitely do that, but not like this. Not without a plan to overpower their captors. She had to intervene before Isaiah did something stupid.

"Isaiah, help me pack the sleeping bags. You know we need to hurry." She searched his intense, fury-filled gaze, pleading with her own.

Rhea approached and leaned into Zach, kissing him and turning his head. Heidi sighed with relief and gestured for Isaiah to join her.

Isaiah climbed inside the tent with Heidi and they started packing up the bags and gear as quickly as possible.

"What were you doing back there?" Heidi hissed.

"You know we're in the best place to wait out

a blizzard for miles. This isn't over yet. Not by a long shot. That's why we brought the tents and food and water. We knew it was coming. So what are you doing, giving in to him?"

Heidi stopped rolling up the bag and looked into Isaiah's eyes. Something pinged in her heart—she'd missed seeing him at the Mountain Cove Avalanche Center ever since they had traded shifts and no longer worked together. Especially his eyes. The contrast of the striking hazel color with his dark brown hair, and the essence of all that was Isaiah in the depths of his gaze, stirred a crazy longing. But it also stirred other emotions like sadness. Regret.

She shoved those unbidden and unwelcome thoughts aside. "We have to pick our battles with Zach. We can't just survive the storm. We have to survive him and his friends. I don't know about the others, but I know Rhea is crazy. My guess is a person would have to be a certain kind of irrational to commit a crime like that. I wouldn't want to risk setting any of them off."

Her throat constricted. She reached toward Isaiah, pressing her hand against his heart. "Please, I couldn't bear it if something happened to either you or Cade. Keep your head down and do what Zach asks us to do. Get them through the mountains so we can go home."

Remorse burned in his eyes. He pressed both

hands over hers on his chest. "I didn't mean to scare you. You're right." He grinned. "You always are. I shouldn't cause any trouble that could get you hurt."

Heidi returned his smile, wishing they were anywhere but here. She had so much to say. So many questions. But the side of her heart that had gone dark over the past few months rebuffed her for giving a possible romantic relationship with Isaiah another thought.

He inched closer. "As much as I hate scaring you, I need to say this. You know they're not going to let us go home. They can't let us go."

Tears burned at the back of her eyes. She hated them. "But they *can*. All we have to do is convince them!"

"That could be a tall order, Heidi, even for you." Isaiah reached up and ran his thumb down her cheek. "You have always been full of hope and life, and able to persuade others to do the impossible. It's what I've always admired about you."

He admires me? How could that be when she'd lost her hope, her love of life? More than anything Heidi wanted to deserve his admiration. She wanted to get back what she'd lost, but how?

Her questions faded with the sear of his touch. She couldn't breathe, but this kind of panic was something much different than her anxiety attacks.

One side of the tent collapsed in on them, jerking her back to reality.

"Hey!" Isaiah yelled.

"What's going on in there?" Cade peeked inside. "Get the bags and get out. You're wasting time."

Heidi didn't recall ever seeing Cade that haggard, well, except after Dad had died in an avalanche. That had been tough on all of them. But Cade had been through something terrifying before when Leah, who had since become his wife, had been stalked by a police detective.

Exiting the tent, Heidi realized everyone had already packed up—and they were waiting on her and Isaiah. Had everyone been listening in on them? Isaiah's words of admiration still burned inside her heart—he was talking about the old Heidi. That person was long dead.

Still, Isaiah made Heidi want that person back. She wanted her old self to live again.

She wanted to survive this and somehow, someway, she had to convince Zach to let them go. He watched her, an uncanny look in his eyes as if he knew what she was thinking.

An arctic gust rippled across her, reminding her that she would only get the chance to convince Zach to let them live if they survived nature's worst.

Isaiah's gut churned. The deep snow became an obstacle course even with snowshoes. A person had to be in great shape to negotiate this terrain and the journey was quickly wearing on their so-called climbers as they all tried to keep up with Cade. They'd descended the ridge without incident and now hiked through a snow-filled gap. At least they were heading into the lower elevations, but not fast enough.

Isaiah expected the weather to worsen again before it got better. Jason followed Cade, then came Liam and Rhea. Heidi hiked behind them, and Isaiah was right behind her.

Zach followed them all, never letting them forget that he was looking for a reason to shoot someone. Anyone. Isaiah tried to keep his head down and simply follow through with the task, but he was constantly formulating escape plans. He bet that Cade and Heidi were, too. If only they could get the chance to strategize together. He'd bet that was why Zach kept them apart.

In front of them, Rhea stumbled and sank several feet into the deep snow, letting out a yelp.

"Cade!" Isaiah called for him to stop and

come back to assist. That far ahead, he wouldn't be aware of Rhea's stumble.

When he saw Rhea, Cade scrambled back to help Isaiah pull her out.

"Get back." Zach shoved Isaiah. "Liam and Jason will help her."

Rhea flailed in the snow. "Someone help me out of this." She refused Liam and Jason's help. "Zach, help me!"

But Zach ignored her plea for help. He held his gun ready, presumably in case Cade or Isaiah tried anything. Breathing hard, Rhea finally crawled far enough to lie flat on a section of packed snow.

Then Heidi reached forward and helped Rhea back to her feet. When Rhea was steady, she shoved Heidi to the ground. Eyes wide, Heidi gazed up at Rhea. What kind of person accepted help, then returned the favor with a vindictive act? Isaiah figured Rhea had simply taken out her disappointment and frustration with Zach on Heidi. Weird and perverse.

Isaiah reached for Heidi and assisted her back to her snowshoed feet. He didn't know why, but he tugged her to him and held tight. "How are you holding up?"

Stupid question.

Wearing a deep frown, Cade headed back to the front of the pack.

She squeezed harder. "I'm okay."

Zach pulled her away from Isaiah and gestured for Isaiah to get going. "Go on. I'll watch over her."

Heidi's eyes narrowed, and Isaiah couldn't stand the dread he saw there. But she gave a subtle shake of her head. She wanted him to comply so there wouldn't be more trouble.

He grabbed the bag he'd dropped, as did Heidi. All the gear and packs they carried, and some they pulled, made their journey sluggish in the loose snow. They were all loaded down like packing mules. It couldn't be helped.

What he wouldn't give for a pair of skis right now.

Or even better, for his weapon back.

"Get going." Zach started forward, and Isaiah took his place in front of him. He didn't miss the murderous look in Rhea's gaze as she watched Zach with Heidi.

Was that for Zach or Heidi?

In the foreboding environment, time seemed to stand still, making it appear as if they hadn't made any progress at all through the gap. But they pressed on anyway, finally reaching a wide opening where they could see for miles. Then, just as Isaiah feared, the wind picked up to a fierce tempo, swirling blinding snow in their paths, and all around them. Isaiah couldn't see in front of him or behind him.

They were going to lose each other forever.

At one point, Isaiah looked up to see nothing but blinding white erasing any sense of sky or earth or horizon. Vertigo knocked him to his knees. Zach and Heidi stumbled over him into the snow. He gripped Heidi's hand. If they made a run for it, even if they couldn't see where they were going, at least they would be free from Zach.

Pulling her to her feet, Isaiah took off. But Zach toppled him, and even in the blizzard the man wouldn't give up his fight, pressing his weapon into Isaiah's temple. "I should shoot you right here."

"Do it. Go ahead and do it! We're all going to die anyway," Isaiah yelled over the storm. "We can't see where we're going. I told you this would happen. You're insane."

Cade pulled Zach off and got in Isaiah's face. "We don't have time for this. We're going to die if we don't stick together through this storm."

"What should we do?" Heidi yelled. "It's a complete whiteout!"

"We stop here." Cade grabbed Zach by the collar. "We'll never make it through this."

"How do we put up the tents now?" Zach

stumbled back, snow sticking to his cheeks and eyebrows. "What about a snow cave?"

"No!" Cade and Isaiah said at the same time.

"You and your men build snow walls like I showed you last night," Isaiah said, "while Cade, Heidi and I set up the tents. We can do it quickly."

Zach shook his head. He wasn't buying it.

"Look, every second you wait we're all getting closer to death. Hypothermia is a real threat. Rhea looks like she's already there. You have no choice."

The man had to admit Isaiah was right. The group huddled together in a circle while the blinding blizzard that left them unable to distinguish anything, causing them to lose all sense of balance, roared around them. Jason fell to his knees.

"Where's Liam?" Zach asked.

"Liam!" Isaiah called.

Zach started to walk away, but Isaiah grabbed him back.

"No. You'll get lost, too, if you go after him. We'll shout his name and if he's out there, he'll find us. Start building the wall right here, which is probably not the best place, but it's all we have."

"Everyone, pile your bags and packs right here in one place so we don't lose anything."

"Heidi and Rhea, you guys dig us out as we go."

As long as they kept moving and built the tents and then stayed inside they had a chance.

"With Liam gone, we don't need that extra tent," Cade said. "Let's just put up two for now so we can get inside and get warm and out of this storm."

A half hour later, Isaiah lay on top of a sleeping bag, exhausted, knowing he would have to exit the warmth of the tent every few minutes—although they would take turns—to dig out the shelters to keep from being buried alive.

"I can't feel my toes," Jason said.

"Get out of your boots. Your sock could be wet. We'll get you warmed up," Heidi said. "This small stove, along with our bodies, will raise the temperature inside."

Isaiah opened the vents to release any carbon monoxide. Though it was a low-output stove designed for this kind of usage, he dug around in the pack for the CO detector.

So far no one had gotten frostbite, but that could easily change. Getting inside and warm would go a long way toward preventing those kinds of injuries.

As Isaiah watched Heidi melt snow in a pan

on the little stove, his heart filled with warmth. He was relieved to be sharing a tent with her and Jason this time. Rhea had insisted she stay with Zach, and he wouldn't allow the rescue team their own tent, of course, leaving Jason to guard Heidi and Isaiah, which meant Cade was with Zach and Rhea.

Isaiah wouldn't try anything. He didn't have the energy to fight the man. He had to conserve everything to battle the storm. To keep Heidi alive. He didn't care about himself or anyone else. Cade could take care of himself, and likely Heidi, too, but making Heidi his mission would keep Isaiah going.

There was a time he thought he could have something with Heidi, but he didn't deserve her and now it seemed it wouldn't matter. Except he'd come too far, moving to a new place and changing his name, to lose it all now to this insanity. But he'd do what it took to keep her alive, even if no one else survived.

She glanced up at him, that small smile he loved on her lips. His pulse jumped. He hadn't seen that in so long, and hadn't realized how much he'd missed it. He hated that she was in the middle of this nightmarish rescue, but in her smile, he saw some small part of the Heidi he'd known before the ordeal of last summer that had changed everything for her.

The thought of how he'd distanced himself after they'd grown close slashed his insides. And then she'd needed him after the accident, but he'd failed her. He should have been there for her, but getting close again would only risk hurting her in the long run.

"Here, drink this. It'll warm you up." She passed the cup to him.

Their fingers brushed. "Thanks."

He was all too aware of their proximity. Did she feel it, too? And even if she did, he wasn't sure what difference that made. He'd already decided she was off-limits to him. Had already put the wall up between them. He could almost be grateful for the raging blizzard outside, and the unintentional chaperone and criminal sharing the tent.

He sipped the warm liquid from the cup, but Heidi did much more to warm his insides. Maybe being in the tent with her hadn't been a good idea. A guy could only control his emotions so much. But he felt better knowing she was safe for the moment, and that was in line with his mission.

Jason drank up as well, and dozed in the corner, barely holding his weapon within reach. Some kind of guard he was. Still, this wasn't the optimal situation for any of them to perform well in. And what did it matter if Isaiah wrestled the gun from him if they all died in the blizzard?

Finishing his drink, Isaiah pulled his gloves back on and shrugged into his coat, tugging the hood over the knit cap he'd switched out with his helmet. "I'm going to dig us out."

Isaiah stepped outside, the shock of cold and snow jolting him as though he hadn't been prepared for it. He began the laborious task of removing the snow and caught a glimpse of Cade doing the same for the tent next door. Any other time, this would have been fortuitous—the two of them outside and alone. They could make plans. But there was no way to do that now.

Over by the snow wall that buffered the wind, the snow had already piled high over their bags. Another bag lay a few feet away, an odd look about it.

Isaiah trudged over. Grabbing the bag, he tried to tug it back with the rest. It rolled over. Liam's stone-cold frozen face stared back.

SEVEN

Stretching, Heidi blinked, her mind slowly registering the gray of morning filtering through the tent.

And something else.

It was quiet. The wind had ceased to snarl around them. The storm had stopped.

Sitting up, she glanced about the tent. Jason stopped snoring and shifted, but Isaiah was gone. He'd already gotten up and out without disturbing the man guarding him.

Peeling out of the sleeping bag, Heidi crawled over and unzipped the tent.

"Where do you think you're going?" Jason grumbled. "Hey, where is everybody?"

Heidi hesitated, then turned to look at him. "I think everyone is packing up. And I think the storm might be over."

Relief washed over Jason's face. He blew out a breath. "Almost dying in a plane crash was bad enough. I don't want to go through any more of these storms."

Compassion kindled in Heidi. "I'm sorry you had to go through that. You know, this probably won't be the only storm we wait out, but we'll try to get you to the ice field as fast as we can."

He nodded, and got out of his sleeping bag.

Heidi zipped the tent completely closed. If she couldn't persuade Zach, maybe she would bring Jason over to her way of thinking. He seemed to have warmed to her. "And if we do that, Zach is going to let us go, right? I mean, a deal is a deal."

Shrugging, he averted his gaze.

Disappointment swelled inside her. She'd try another tact. "How did you get involved with him anyway?"

Jason swiped his light brown hair from his face and narrowed his eyes. His cheeks were puffy and red, and his expression reminded her of a young child. "I didn't wake up one morning and decide I wanted to rob an armored car, if that's what you think. But I'm in it now, and Zach is calling the shots. He's just crazy enough that I have no intention of offering up information like I did before. You can quit with your interrogation."

So he wouldn't be so easily persuaded to share what he knew about Zach's plans.

Heidi ignored her disappointment. "No interrogation. But even though you somehow got in with Zach, it doesn't mean you have to keep going down this road. You have choices, you know?"

"That's easy for you to say. I got no more choice right now than you do."

"Why do you say that?"

"I'm not talking to you anymore." His gun within easy reach, Jason pulled on his boots, shuffled around, found his coat and gloves, and donned them, as well.

When he started for the tent exit, Heidi moved aside and let him go through first. Well, it had been worth a shot. Still, she'd seen something behind his eyes. He wasn't as hard-hearted as he wanted her to believe. Everyone, even bad guys, had something good inside of them. Maybe Heidi was crazy to believe the way she did, but she hoped to find Jason's soft spot and connect that way. It might be their only chance.

Heidi started out of the tent only to face Isaiah on his way in, his nearness taking her breath, like always. She scooted out of his way.

"What's going on out there?" she asked. "Where did you go?"

"The sky's clear for now." A grin crept into his somber expression. "It's going to be a sunny day."

"Oh, Isaiah." Relief swept over her. But they

weren't out of this yet. "I'm amazed we made it this far. But that still doesn't answer my question."

He started rolling up the bags. "I went to explore what we'd face next, see where we've been and where we need to go. I didn't go far."

"And nobody saw you? Stopped you?"

He shook his head. "Everyone is too exhausted. These guys aren't accustomed to this much exertion. Frankly, neither am I."

He sent her a wry grin, along with a chuckle.

"Why didn't you try to get a radio and make a call for help?"

Pausing, he looked up at her. "How do you know I didn't?"

Words caught in her throat. She studied him, her heart pounding. "Did you?"

He focused on the sleeping bags again. "I tried. Couldn't get through."

"Isaiah, what if Zach had caught you?" She crawled closer. "He'll kill you if he finds out."

He started to speak, but she pressed her hand over his mouth. "Don't say he's going to kill us anyway. I don't want to hear it. There has to be another way. I talked to Jason this morning."

Isaiah scowled. "You're not going to talk us out of this. Jason is not going to help us."

"Then why don't we overpower them, get the guns back? Something." She hated the trembling that crept into her voice along with a rising panic.

"If we get the chance, we will. But I need to tell you something." Isaiah gripped her shoulders.

"What is it? Is it Cade?" *Oh, God, please no...*

"No, no." He hesitated, then, "I found Liam's body yesterday." Another pause, then, "I haven't told anyone yet."

Heidi shrank back, tears surging. She'd presumed he'd died. They all had. How could he have survived out there? But to find his body...

Covering her mouth, she sobbed softly. Isaiah pulled her to him and held her. His arms felt strong around her, and she could easily sink into his chest and soak up his confidence, his reassurance. Everything about Isaiah that she admired. And Heidi wanted so much more from him, but she couldn't bear the thought of getting hurt again. Isaiah had been the first one to hurt her. He'd been the one to start her spiral away from trusting in forever, and he'd done it while they were only friends. She couldn't imagine how hard it would be if she let herself love him.

She moved away from his embrace.

"I know the point of search and rescue is to save people," he said. "I don't want to sound harsh, but he might not be the last person to die as we make it through these mountains. Do you understand what I'm saying?"

Heidi nodded. The harsh environment would pick them off, one by one, despite the best efforts of the search and rescue team. Then they could worry about fighting whoever was left. But she didn't get the chance to voice her thoughts.

Outside the tent, someone shouted.

Gunfire resounded through the mountains.

"Stay here." Isaiah scrambled from the tent, praying Zach hadn't suddenly decided to shoot them all now.

Zach stood a few yards away from the tents where Cade and Rhea had paused from digging out the bags. Had he found the body?

The man holding the weapon turned, spotted Isaiah, and the game was over. "There's the man of the hour."

Uh-oh.

Zach strolled toward Isaiah looking as if he would toy with him, maybe even kill him. Isaiah stiffened when Zach looked from the gun to Isaiah. "Rhea said she saw you leave the camp this morning."

"Just scouting around to see where we need to go, that's all."

"With a radio."

"She was mistaken." Isaiah kept his face straight. "Radios don't work out here." Depended on the radio, of course.

Zach shot a look at Rhea. Isaiah feared she would argue with him, try to convince Zach that Isaiah was the liar, but terror filled her eyes instead. The control this guy had over his people should be more than terrifying, but Isaiah hoped to use it to his advantage.

Heidi tromped up behind him.

His gut clenched.

I told you to stay in the tent.

He wanted to whirl on her and send her back, but he stood his ground. Didn't move. Didn't flinch. Didn't act as if he cared.

Unfortunately, that wasn't enough to fool Zach. The smirk that Isaiah was growing to hate filled out Zach's face as he studied Heidi.

"What was with the gunshot?" Isaiah hoped to distract him.

"I fired off a shot to bring you back from wherever you'd gone, and to remind everyone who is in charge. And it worked. You showed up, and everyone is shaking in their snowshoes."

"Come here, sweetheart." Zach motioned for Heidi to come closer.

Isaiah almost threw his arm out to stop her. Push her behind him. But doing that would only put her in more danger. Zach was becoming drunk on his sense of power and the money he lugged around with him. Isaiah had to bide his time until he could take Zach down for good.

Though he hated that someone had died, there was one less person for him to fight. When would Zach bring up his friend? Mourn his loss? Did he even care?

Heidi hiked over to Zach, and Isaiah didn't miss Rhea's hateful look.

Zach snatched her to him. Cade flinched at the same moment Isaiah stepped forward, reacting before he could catch himself. And that was the worst thing he could do. Zach would take that and run with it. Toy with them in painful ways Isaiah didn't want to imagine.

The man pulled her even closer and smelled her hair in an overly dramatic fashion. "I love the smell of lavender."

Zach's gaze stabbed Isaiah. It took everything inside him not to take the bait.

Isaiah clenched his teeth, squeezed his gloved fists and stared Zach down. They would have their moment to face off.

"Rhea, bring me the radio."

Rhea glared at Zach and Heidi, but did as she was told, handing off the device.

Isaiah thought he'd been as discreet as possible earlier when he'd tried to establish radio contact with the command center. Everyone had been snoring. He'd taken a risk, yes, but what else could he do? He'd lied when he'd said the radios don't work here. Sometimes they did. Same with the SAT phones. It all depended on a lot of factors. But he still hadn't been able to reach anyone.

In the silent winter wonderland around him, in the terror of the scenario unfolding, his heartbeat resounded in his ears. Isaiah prayed hard. *God, please. I know what I said earlier, begging You to let the radio work, but I want to reverse that request now.*

Zach tried the radio.

They all listened to the static as the sun peeked over the mountains from the east.

"If we have any chance of making the ice field, we don't have time for games." Cade dug their bags and packs filled with supplies and gear out of the snow. "Like Isaiah said, radios don't always work out here. We're in the mountains in a dead zone."

"Why'd you take the radio, then?"

"I told you, I didn't." Okay, so that was a lie, but it was unavoidable. He stood his ground.

Cutting Zach's interrogation short, Isaiah ignored him and hiked over to help dig their gear out, keeping his head down. Cade was right to bring Zach's focus back. Another storm could come through and bury them for good this time.

They had to make it all the way out of this gap between the mountains that created another ferocious wind tunnel before it began all over again.

When Isaiah knew that Zach had lost interest in grilling him about the radio, or using Heidi to taunt him, he blew out a breath. In his peripheral vision he saw Zach, Jason and Rhea breaking down the tents. He and Cade should do it, to make sure they didn't destroy their only protection against this environment, but he needed a moment to steady his nerves, rein in his anger.

Cade grabbed a snow-covered bag near Isaiah, leaning in. "I'm surprised you held it together."

How well Cade knew him. "Thanks for jumping in when you did."

"The radio wasn't the issue. I jumped in to protect all of us, but especially my sister. It's obvious that Zach has picked up on your affinity for Heidi."

Isaiah shrugged, digging another bag out. "I haven't done anything to encourage him, Cade. You have to know that. I haven't responded to any of his taunts. I wouldn't do that to Heidi. He just doesn't like me. That's all."

Cade's eyes were colder than the air. "You're going to get her killed."

"What do you want me to do? Walk off the

next cliff?" Isaiah wished he could take the words back.

Breathing hard, Cade straightened to his full height. "Just keep your head down and stay out of trouble. Don't leave the camp again. Don't try *anything* again."

"Have you got a plan then? Because I'd sure love to hear it."

"Sure I do. I plan to get the group to safety. We're taking them to the ice field. We have to believe a search and rescue team will find us by then. David will figure out something has gone wrong soon, if he hasn't already."

Isaiah wanted to believe in Cade's plan. He really did. "This guy isn't going to let them find us, and besides, we have to warn them, Cade. We can't allow more people to be put in danger."

Since Cade was clearly delusional, finding a way out of this mess was up to Isaiah.

EIGHT

They hiked in snowshoes throughout the morning, but at least the sun broke through the clouds and warmed them, though Heidi knew that another snowstorm was on the way. And when it came, the inclement weather would be like a recurring nightmare. Torturing them during the day, too.

Facing the harsh Alaska environment was one thing, but she'd never imagined herself in this predicament. Not in her worst nightmares, recurring or not. This journey couldn't end soon enough. And yet she almost dreaded the end, especially after Isaiah's words.

They can't let us go.

Would she face her death, then? Watch Cade and Isaiah be executed?

Heidi shoved aside the foreboding thoughts, though they stayed at the edge of her mind. She wished she were hiking closer to Cade and Isaiah. Instead, Zach kept her near him at the back of the line so he could use her to control them. Cade led the way as they hiked out and down toward the base of the mountain, followed by Jason, Isaiah, Rhea and then Zach with Heidi.

Rhea tried to hang back so she could be near Zach, the man she claimed to love, but he kept urging her forward. If only he would pay attention to Rhea and reassure her of his affections. After her talk with Rhea, Heidi hoped she'd convinced the woman she had no plans to steal Zach away. The very idea made her shudder.

"What's going through that pretty head of yours?" he asked.

His question repulsed her. Rhea glanced back and glared at Heidi.

"I'm thinking about what's up ahead. We got a short reprieve from stormy weather and from any serious climbing. But there's more to come. And we're all exhausted." How would they survive this?

"Those energy bars don't stay with you long, do they? I'm hungry again. Aren't you?" Zach's attempt at a normal conversation fell flat. What did he think? That he could change the way Heidi thought of him?

"Yeah, I'm hungry, too," she admitted. They were burning up their energy reserves quickly, and running out of supplies.

Rhea slowed and hiked next to them, and this

time, Zach said nothing about it. "Do you think we'll need to use your climbing ropes again?" she asked. "That was the worst experience of my life."

Heidi nodded, pleased that Rhea's thoughts were now turned to the dangers ahead, and not Zach's misconstrued interest in Heidi. At least she hoped Zach had no real interest in her. She ignored any warning thoughts to the contrary, burying them deep.

"Mine, too. But we won't have to climb at night during a storm if Zach doesn't force us to."

She hoped Zach wouldn't push them, if it came to that.

At her comment, he scowled at Rhea. "Get back up there, you're slowing us down." Once again he urged Rhea ahead.

By the time the sun had crawled to late morning, almost lunch, Heidi's stomach had been rumbling for over an hour. They only had a few energy bars left and would need to save them, or else start on the MREs. David would be expecting them to show up where Isaiah had said they would be hiking down, but he'd been forced to misdirect the rest of the team who presumably waited back at the command center. How long before David sent helicopters out to search for them? Would they look for them in this region, and could they even spot them if they did?

She felt Zach's eyes on her. She had no doubt he would force them to hide. But maybe a helicopter would spot their tracks before the next storm came through.

Please, God...

Ahead of them, Cade stopped, his rigid form reminding her of their traumatic scale down the ridge two nights ago, only this morning they wouldn't have to use their night vision goggles. The group crowded together near the edge of a jagged escarpment.

No one said a word, but their shared dread was palpable.

"Why did you lead us this way?" Zach shoved Cade.

"It doesn't matter which way we go, we're descending from the mountain summit. That will involve a combination of hiking and rappelling. No way around it. You wanted to make the ice field, this is the only way. It was your decision to put fast over safe."

Venom filled Zach's laugh.

"Look at it this way." Isaiah dropped his backpack. "It will be a breeze compared to the last time we did this."

Exactly the way Heidi saw it. The only difference was these guys could now see what they were facing and they might panic or cause problems.

Whimpering, Rhea covered her mouth. "I can't do that! Not again. Please, don't make us do this, Zach."

Heidi's heart went out to the woman. She had panicked the first time she'd been assisted down a ridge, and she hadn't been able to see into the dark abyss beneath her. Now she had to be a hundred times more terrified.

"Shut up. We don't have a choice."

"The burden is on us," Heidi said. "We're the experienced climbers, so you don't have to do anything but trust us. Just like last time."

In a way, the power now shifted back to the search and rescue team. A tenuous smile crept onto Heidi's lips. She hadn't meant for the words to give her any sense of power, but they had all the same. She dropped her backpack and gear and moved to stand next to Cade and Isaiah. Unfortunately, Zach didn't let her stray too far from him.

"So what are we doing? Same as last time?" Isaiah asked.

"No other choice." Cade searched for an anchor point. "Anything else and people die."

That odd sense that things were not right with the world dinged her thoughts. They were working hard to assist this group safely down a mountain—a group that had every intention of killing them when it was over. Insanity ruled the day.

Heidi sighed and gazed down the gash in the valley of the mountain fold they'd been following. They were tiny, insignificant creatures in this wild topography. "It's going to be close. That's a long drop. Our rope needs to be twice that length."

Isaiah flicked his gaze to Zach. The look in his eyes chilled her more than the icy landscape. "Doesn't matter. We're going down."

Dropping his backpack and gear, Zach shifted uncomfortably. Had it occurred to him that the SAR team might attempt to deliver him down the escarpment in a risky fashion, ensuring their own safety?

"I'm heading down and will receive the packages." Geared up to rappel, Cade dropped out of sight.

Rhea's face paled. Maybe she didn't like being referred to as a package.

Isaiah pulled out the seat harness they'd created from the tubular webbing. They would then lower Zach and his friends the entire distance, though, like Heidi said, it was going to be close. Heidi set up the anchor point for the operation and clipped in the carabiner for the belay device. She was vaguely aware of Jason, Zach and Rhea watching as she and Isaiah prepared everything to lower them. Were they aware of the fact they were putting their lives in search and rescue team's hands? The very team that they had abducted? The whole thing was surreal.

Heidi barely registered that Rhea had meandered over to where she worked. She glanced up and something in Rhea's eyes made Heidi take a step away from the staggering, jagged-edged drop-off.

Rhea bumped into her.

Hard.

More like shoved.

Heidi teetered before stumbling into a granite boulder that broke through the snow. Her heart jumped to her throat, lodged there and pounded. She could have gone over the edge, falling hundreds of feet to her death.

Had that been Rhea's intention?

Her knees screaming, Heidi wanted to cry out, too, but stifled her reaction. She rolled away from the rock into the soft snow, praying she wasn't too injured to hike out, or else Zach would kill her. Of that she had no doubt.

She'd slow them down, and he wouldn't accept that. He'd made that plain enough when he'd killed one of his own people.

"What was that for?" she asked.

Rhea leaned over her. "I warned you to stay

away from him. Next time, I'll make sure to shove you off a cliff."

Heidi gasped. "I've already told you I have no interest in him. He's a criminal, and he's all yours."

Rhea's frown deepened as though she considered Heidi's remark an insult. Heidi hadn't intended it as such; she was simply stating the facts. Rhea could take it however she wanted.

Gripping her knees, she glanced up to notice Zach watching the two of them from where he stood at the ledge. She forced a straight face, hoping to hide her pain, and attempted to stand, but fell back in the snow. His face pale and drained, he hiked over. Maybe that was from watching Jason being lowered down the ledge. Served him right.

"What are you two doing over here?" He directed his harsh tone at Rhea. "You need to pay attention to what's going on, so you don't get yourself killed. Got it?"

Rhea shrank away from him, then glared at Heidi as if Zach's scolding was her fault. The woman opened her mouth to speak, but then Zach grabbed Heidi's hand and assisted her up, a concerned smile on his face. Was he for real?

Not good. Not good at all.

Heidi hadn't done anything to garner his attention or smile. Couldn't Rhea see that? But his beam didn't win Heidi any points with Rhea. And this time, he didn't appear to be using her as a way of taunting Isaiah or her brother. But she'd buried her fear that he might actually be attracted to her and instead hoped and prayed he was simply using her as a pawn.

Back on her feet, Heidi saw that Isaiah had turned from the edge of the escarpment and spotted the three of them. The power of his dark gaze crossed the distance and held her.

Oh, Lord, please don't let him interfere. Or try something that would get him killed. She wouldn't put it past him to risk it all to save her. Funny to think that even though Cade was her brother, and an overprotective one at that, it was Isaiah who was acting this way. And something in Isaiah's fierce watchfulness ignited her feelings for him—emotions she'd tried to keep buried. She missed their easy friendship, and wished he hadn't pushed her away. But even if he hadn't, Heidi couldn't trust anyone with her heart.

She'd keep telling herself that. Except, as she watched Isaiah moving toward them, she knew if she could trust anyone with her heart, she'd want that someone to be Isaiah. Good thing her mind reigned over her heart.

And then he stood there in the mix—between

her and Rhea and Zach. Heidi admitted his presence brought a measure of relief.

"Isaiah." She exhaled his name.

Her mind and heart battled for control.

Now she understood how Rhea had known Heidi cared for Isaiah. Hopefully Rhea would see that again now, just a little, but if she recognized it, then unfortunately, Zach would, too.

As if he answered Isaiah's unspoken but tangible challenge, Zach stood taller, the exhaustion in his features morphing into aggression.

Somehow Heidi had to defuse the explosive tension, and fast.

"What's going on here?" An idiot could see that Heidi was hurt. "You guys need to get ready for the ride down."

Isaiah knew not to draw attention to the fact that Heidi was somehow injured—if Zach didn't already know. Heidi succumbing to an injury could lead to the criminal-in-charge putting her out of her misery. Isaiah had every intention of facing off with the maniac right here and now if that's what it came to. After all, half the men were at the base of the cliff. Isaiah could take Zach down if he could separate him from his weapons.

True to form, Zach tugged the gun from his

pocket and pointed it at Heidi. Would he do this every time?

Isaiah threw up his hands in surrender and took a step back. "Whoa! Whoa! What are you doing?"

He'd caused Zach's reaction. Why did he always have to be the reason a woman suffered? Heidi blanched, her eyes pleading with Isaiah. Powerless, there was nothing he could do except back off. But more than anything he wanted to take Zach down and bury him deep in the snow, then wrap his arms around Heidi. He wasn't worried about Rhea. As a threat, she was a non-issue.

"Just reminding you who is in charge." Zach's smirk grew broader.

"Put the gun down." Palms down, Isaiah slowly lowered his hands. He knew he'd come on too strong in his attitude. "We need to get going so we don't get caught in another blizzard. We won't make your rendezvous if we do." Isaiah wasn't sure they would make it in time even if they *didn't* catch another storm.

Deep inside, Isaiah wanted to hope, as Cade did, that making the rendezvous would be their freedom. But no matter how hard he tried, he knew it couldn't be true. Weird that they had to rush toward this one goal that would only end their lives. They were running toward death itself.

He glanced at the blue sky. Ominous clouds were building in the distance once again. Why couldn't he hear the welcome sound of rotor blades? David had to suspect something was wrong by now. But then what would Zach do? Hold them hostage?

"Let's do it then." Zach lowered his weapon, though he kept it at his side, and marched to where they'd rigged the ropes. "Just remember, your man Cade is being held at gunpoint at the bottom, should something happen to any of us." The man chuckled. "We're in control. We're always going to be in control. Don't think you can pull a fast one."

Isaiah blew out a breath. He was right, of course. The way things were, they could never gain an advantage. It was too risky to try something that could end in harm to one of them. Right now, guiding these creeps through the mountain wilderness was all they could do. Until their chance for an escape came.

Rhea tossed one last glare at Heidi, and even one at Isaiah, then followed her man to the edge. That's how it would be with her—that is, until Zach had a reason to leave her behind. Isaiah shook his head, and when he thought it was safe—Zach and Rhea were caught up in a conversation of their own—he turned his attention to Heidi. Cade was probably wondering what had happened to Isaiah. They needed to bring the seat harness back up for the next rider.

But Isaiah had to make sure Heidi was all right. Really all right.

She took a limping step toward him, and he closed the distance. Caught her up in his arms. For the briefest of moments he allowed himself to savor the embrace, then he put an arm's-length distance between them, gripping her shoulders.

"Are you okay?" Isaiah pinned her gaze. Searched it. He wanted the truth.

She nodded. "I will be. My knees are bruised, that's all."

He glanced over his shoulder to make sure Zach and Rhea were still occupied. He had to hurry. Cade was waiting on him to manage the rope at this end. "What happened?"

"Rhea. She tried to push me over."

The news stunned Isaiah. So Rhea wasn't a nonissue, after all. Isaiah had to make sure that Heidi wasn't left alone with that woman for even one minute, especially when they set up camp again. He'd make sure he was in the tent, too, to keep them apart.

"Get over here," Zach called, reminding Isaiah that he wasn't in charge and couldn't control if Heidi was left alone with Rhea.

"You know to keep your guard up around her, then."

The words sounded completely lame when all he wanted was to reassure her that he was there for her. But why would he do that now when he hadn't been there for her when she'd needed him those months after the accident? Why would she believe him?

But that's all he could say. He shouldn't make promises that he couldn't keep.

"I know. If I hadn't stepped back when I had then she would have been successful in her attempt." Heidi looked down, sucking in a quick breath. Then another.

Okay. So Isaiah would make those promises now. He couldn't let her fall prey to a panic attack in front of everyone. But he'd made promises before. And someone had died in the end, and all because of him. Isaiah closed his eyes for a split second and buried those thoughts—they wouldn't do him any good here. Wouldn't help Heidi now.

He opened his eyes. "Look at me."

Her gaze drew up to his. Beautiful dark brown eyes, the color of black coffee. He'd been drawn into them the moment he'd met her. What was the matter with him? He couldn't think about that now. "Breathe, just breathe slowly and calmly. I'm here for you. I won't let anyone hurt you."

Pain flickered behind her eyes and knifed through him. He'd caused that pain, and he wouldn't deny his own guilt. "Do you believe me?"

His pulse slowed as if with time—he hadn't realized how important her answer to his question would be. Reluctance surfaced behind those dark irises. Doubt, heavy and suffocating, swirled in them.

Heidi nodded slowly. *She nodded.*

Isaiah couldn't believe it. Why was she lying? But maybe, just as he *wanted* her to trust him, she *wanted* to trust him, despite his actions in the past. Despite the fact that he'd severed their emotional connection just as it had grown strong. Maybe she was simply taking a leap of faith.

"We'd better get those two down the cliff before Zach gets crazy and does something stupid." She stepped away from Isaiah, freeing herself from his grip and standing tall despite her injury.

Good. She was breathing okay now, too. Heidi was a strong woman, and Isaiah didn't doubt that for a minute, but this situation pushed each of them to the edge, and would likely test their limits before it was over.

NINE

Isaiah grimaced. Rhea screamed all the way down as they lowered her. Just like last time, only much worse. Her screams echoed through the mountains. Were there any searchers out there to hear her?

Cade and Jason signaled from below when Rhea was safely at the bottom, and Isaiah pulled the rope and harness back up. He glanced at Zach.

"You're next."

"What, and leave you and her here to run off? Not going to happen."

The last time, Isaiah and Heidi had rappelled after the last person was lowered. But Zach wasn't willing to trust them this time.

"Look, man, we're not going to leave Cade behind. We're not running off. You don't have a choice, unless you can climb."

"I can."

Suspicion crawled over Isaiah. As if he

needed another reason to be wary of this man. He shared a look with Heidi. Zach had kept silent about his skills, keeping it from the SAR team and his partners. What was the man up to? "Why didn't you say something before?" What other skills did he possess? Maybe he really knew how to handle that gun.

"There was no call. I couldn't scale the mountain that night without goggles anyway."

True, all true. That had been one of the toughest mountain-climbing experiences of Isaiah's life. But he suspected the man had other reasons for keeping his climbing skills to himself. Whatever his reasons, the others would find out now.

"So you're next, and I'll rap down with Heidi last."

Isaiah's chest squeezed. Maybe this is how it felt for Heidi when she couldn't breathe. No way would he let that happen. He stepped in front of her, blocking Zach's view. "That's not how it's going to be. I don't know how strong of a climber you are. It's you and me."

On that point Isaiah wouldn't give. Setting his face like flint, he made sure Zach felt it in his gaze. Zach fingered the weapon in his pocket, but his hesitation was evident.

Heidi moved from behind him, and Isaiah instinctively knew she wanted to protest. She, in fact, was the better climber. He thrust his hand back and gripped her arm, willing her to stay still, to understand.

"You and me then."

"But—" Heidi stepped forward.

"You take the harness and we'll drop you down, Heidi." It was quicker and Isaiah didn't want to give Zach a chance to change his mind.

Heidi's expression told him she didn't like the way he'd handled this, but neither of them wanted to argue in front of their mutual enemy. After she was secured in the harness, Isaiah and Cade worked to lower her. There just wasn't enough rope to do it any other way. This was what it felt like to not be in control of your life. He'd much rather cling to the mountain—feel the grip of solid rock beneath his fingers. Somehow, he was sure Heidi felt the same way. Especially when he caught her glance up at him, the fear tracing across her face.

Then it was time for Isaiah to see just what skills Zach had to offer. And it was time for Isaiah to ask the question that had been burning in his gut from the beginning.

He reworked the ropes so he and Zach could rappel, bringing the rope down with them as they went.

"Why'd you do it? Why'd you commit a robbery?" And how much money had he robbed? Had to be a lot if it was an armored car.

Zach looked surprised at his question. "Why do you want to know?"

They started down, Isaiah first, setting the rappel stations, and Zach following. This might be the only time he had the guy alone. "I'm not sure how to explain that."

Despite the temperatures and the snow and ice, the sun warmed him beneath his coat. "You'll be on the run for the rest of your life," he added.

As he rappelled, he gained clarity in his thoughts and emotions. The fresh air and exhilarating climb pushed adrenaline through him. He found the reason and held on to it. He wanted to understand because, in a way, he was like Zach. Isaiah was running, too, only he hadn't committed a crime. But that hadn't seemed to matter. People were suspicious of him all the same, and it had been enough to ruin his life. Make his neighbors and friends wary of him in the small Montana town where the murder had occurred.

He would never have chosen to leave, if not for those circumstances out of his control. And yet, it had been within his power to stop. He'd veered slightly and that small tangent had taken him far off track.

Zach grunted above him, making his way down. He hadn't answered Isaiah yet. Maybe he'd never considered the question, or never thought that it would be asked. But when he drew near so Isaiah could hear, he answered.

"I was a nobody from nowhere, that's why. Nobody paid me any attention—that is, until I started planning the heist. Now I have Rhea, a beautiful woman, by my side. And she's jealous of Heidi."

Now Isaiah understood. Zach was using Heidi for more than leverage against him and Cade. But the way he said it, Isaiah knew the man believed that Heidi returned his attraction.

Isaiah would never purposefully harm someone, though he'd been questioned by the police for the murder of a woman he loved, but anger burned so deep, and protectiveness ignited so bright, that he could almost imagine himself causing Zach to fall to his death. He reined in the thoughts, knowing that God was watching. Always watching. And that wasn't the way to handle their predicament.

He hadn't been able to prevent Leslie's murder. God help him, but he wanted to protect Heidi.

He should have done something to protect Leslie when it became clear that her fiancé had a violent history. But what? The police hadn't listened when it mattered.

And this time, even with God looking on,

would he have to actually kill someone to protect another?

At the bottom of the cliff, Heidi watched Isaiah and Zach scale the cliff face, grateful that snow and ice hadn't clung to the rocks on this side. She'd been as stunned as Isaiah at the news that Zach could climb. But right now, her pulse thrummed in her neck—would Zach do something to harm Isaiah? The man had seemed to look for a reason to hurt Isaiah from the beginning.

Not to mention that Isaiah had stood up to Zach moments ago and Zach had backed down. Would he want to exact some sort of twisted revenge?

Cade discussed their path to the ice field with Jason, while Rhea sat on the bags, nursing her imaginary wounds from the trauma of being lowered to the bottom. She ranted, going on about how she hated amusement parks. Could never ride the roller coasters. That this had been the worst day of her life.

Granted it was quite a breathtaking drop, and Heidi understood Rhea's pain. But, though Heidi hadn't liked sitting in the seat harness either, she couldn't help but harbor some satisfaction in Rhea's discomfort, and smiled to herself before glancing back up to Isaiah.

Even in April, the days weren't that long, and especially up here, the sun dipped below the mountain range far too early. High in the sky, the sun now prevented her from seeing Isaiah, so she moved closer, into the shadows of the cliff he rappelled.

Isaiah and Zach. What an odd pair they made.

They were moving at a good pace and worked together as though they'd been doing this for years.

"Come on, Isaiah, slow and steady," she whispered under her breath.

I'm here for you. I won't let anyone hurt you. The moment he'd said those words they'd wrapped around her and squeezed, sending her heart and mind back into a raging battle. Oh, how she wished those words were true, that she could count on him, could trust him. He cared about her—she'd seen it in his eyes—and yet he'd been the one to sever whatever connection they'd had together. And Heidi had experienced too much heartbreak since then. There was enough hurt and pain in the world, and she wouldn't subject herself to it ever again.

Hot tears surged in the corners of her eyes.

Oh, not now. Not now! She refused to swipe at them and give herself away. In her peripheral vision, she saw Rhea push from the bags and meander toward her. Not again. Heidi didn't want to talk to the woman. Why did she have to be fixated on Heidi? For that matter, why did Zach have to be fixated on her? Heidi kept her focus on the two men almost down the rock-faced cliff.

Zach had made Rhea hate Heidi with his smiles and attention. If only there was a way that Heidi could avoid interacting with either of them, but Rhea had given her those creepy eyes from the first moment she'd seen her. That should have been warning enough. Now she was making her way over to Heidi.

"How are your knees?"

The gall.

"They're fine. I'm fine."

"Could have been worse." Rhea laughed her deep, hoarse laugh. The laugh of a smoker.

Yeah. Thanks for nothing. Heidi didn't appreciate her facetious jab at almost killing her. *God, what do I say to this woman? What do I do?*

Hiking in this terrain was no easy task, and if Rhea was a smoker she had to be struggling. Even though she'd wanted to avoid Rhea altogether, Heidi turned to her. "How are you holding up? This has to be really hard for you."

And she meant the words. Would Rhea see that? The woman studied Heidi, searched her gaze as though she wanted to believe her. Heidi recognized the questions in Rhea's eyes. How could Heidi sincerely care about Rhea? How could she be sympathetic or wish her well? In truth, Heidi struggled with those same questions, but she reminded herself that Rhea was misguided. How would she ever make it off the wrong path if no one stopped to show her the way?

For an instant, Heidi thought Rhea trusted her, had received her kindness. But if she had, even for a moment, Rhea hid it behind her narrowing gaze.

"Oh, you're good, really good. Trying to make me think you care." Rhea hiked away from Heidi toward Zach, who'd finished his climb down. She glanced back at Heidi. "You watch your back."

Why had she wasted her breath on that woman? Bile rose in her throat—she hated her reaction to Rhea's threat, but couldn't overcome it.

Carrying the ropes and gear, Isaiah hiked toward Heidi, his tall frame and lithe form filling her vision, and unfortunately making her heart swell. Heidi imagined they were in another time and place and Isaiah caught her up in his arms. But that was in a world where people didn't cheat on each other, didn't forsake each other. That wasn't this world.

I'm here for you. I won't let anyone hurt you.

But you *hurt me, Isaiah. You.*

Even though Isaiah's look begged her to believe in him, she allowed the sound of Cade's voice calling her name to cut through the power that held her there, and she turned her back on Isaiah.

TEN

With only a few hours left in the day, they pressed on, making as much headway as they could while light remained. Isaiah leaned his head back, gleaning a little warmth from the sun as it broke through one of the few clouds skittering across the heavens. It almost seemed strange to finally see deep blue sky after the bombardment of storms they'd been through. So far the clouds had abated, and the group was left to trudge toward their ominous destination without any hitches.

Once again, Cade led the pack, not that Isaiah resented him. Cade had grown up in the region, knew everything there was to know about it, even the coastal range that bordered with Canada.

Isaiah thought back to his disagreement with Cade, who wanted to deliver this group to the ice field and hope for the best. He wasn't up for risking an escape or going for the guns. He

believed David would send a SAR team to find
them, and would probably be among the searchers himself. Adam, too. Isaiah prayed for the
best outcome, too, but he wasn't one to do nothing if there was another way. At least he and
Cade could search for that way out, but it looked
as if Cade was given to his own plan. The guy
hadn't said two words to Isaiah since their disagreement. Not that there was much opportunity
for conversation with a killer pressing at their
backs. But Cade had been more aloof with Isaiah, tossing him cold, accusing stares. Willing
Isaiah to follow his lead and not stir up trouble
for them.

He had a point on that. Isaiah didn't want
more trouble.

Sounded as if Zach had enough trouble within
his own ranks, though. The killer, who was pulling up the rear, was engaged in a disagreement
with his cohorts.

Unfortunately, Heidi trailed Isaiah, forcing her to walk closer to crazy Zach and his
girlfriend, who looked a little off, too. But a
glance behind him told Isaiah that Heidi no longer walked next to Zach, who had slowed even
more to argue with Rhea.

Isaiah had made Heidi a promise. He had the
gut feeling it was a promise she didn't want,
maybe didn't need, but he was more worried it

was a promise he couldn't keep. Regardless, he'd made it—and Heidi had no idea what drove him to want to protect her. She could never know.

Isaiah suspected the reasons went much deeper than the trauma of his past. Even if he hadn't been close to a murder victim, blamed himself for her death and been considered a person of interest, he would have made the promise to Heidi.

There. He admitted it. Felt good, too.

He'd forced emotional distance between them to protect her from him, and to protect himself. But more often than not, he wondered if that had been a mistake. He couldn't deny he was drawn to her and every time she looked at him he saw the hurt in her eyes, though it decreased every day.

She was getting over the hurt. That was a good thing, wasn't it?

Yes and no. Isaiah couldn't help but feel the pain of loss. But none of that mattered in this insanity. What mattered was that Isaiah would protect Heidi. He'd never doubted that, but now he'd voiced the words to her, and that made her even more vulnerable because she might just trust him enough to follow through.

Sure, she could hold her own, and true, her brother Cade would do anything it took to keep his sister safe, but Isaiah wanted her to know he was there for her, too. He would make a difference when it counted. He *had* to make a difference this time.

Isaiah had been hiking fast enough to keep up with Cade's relentless pace, but Isaiah slowed, letting Heidi catch up with him. She kept her head down for the most part, focusing on putting one foot in front of the other. This was an endurance test they would all have to pass.

Behind them, Rhea continued to argue with Zach. Jason grumbled, as well. When Heidi looked up at Isaiah, he recognized the concern in her eyes over the discontent among the criminals. He felt it, too.

What would their grumbling mean for Cade, Isaiah and Heidi?

Isaiah slowed down even more to see if he could make out their conversation. If there was something other than a field of snow ahead of them, he might suggest that he and Heidi and Cade make a run for it. They could hide. But Cade would likely argue that they might be gunned down before they could ever find cover.

Soon enough, Zach would realize their formation had gone awry and Heidi would likely be in the back with him again, but for now, Isaiah needed to know what they were saying.

"If you can't get ahold of him how do you know he's going to be there?" Jason asked. "He's dumped us, that's what he's done. We're on our own."

"Shut your mouth, do you hear me?" Zach again.

"I'm so tired now. How are we going to make it?" Rhea whined. "Can't you have him pick us up somewhere near here? Get a helicopter or something."

"Both of you, shut your traps."

The pause in conversation implied that they feared Isaiah was listening. Time to redirect things. "Tell me about your photography?"

"Huh?" Heidi stumbled a little.

"We want them to think we're engrossed in our own discussion," he said under his breath.

"Oh, yeah, well, I think photography has kept me sane these past few…" Heidi let her voice trail.

"Months?" he finished for her. He hadn't meant for the conversation to turn serious, but she'd opened that door. "Heidi, I'm so sorry about everything that happened to you." *Including any part I played in it.*

"I didn't think I'd ever get over the day Jenks fell and died. I should have done something to keep it from happening. Some search and rescue team member I am."

"Hey, it wasn't your fault, Heidi. Never was."

He knew others had told her that repeatedly, but she'd been unwilling to accept it.

He wasn't sure he would've reacted any differently had he gone hiking with friends and someone fell to their death. After all, they both assisted people who'd made poor judgment calls and were trapped or lost or injured in the wilderness. To have that happen on her watch had crippled her.

"No point in arguing about whose fault it was," she said. "It happened and it changed me. I'm coping better now. But then came Lon and the fact that he was married."

She conveniently left out that before the accident, and before Lon, Isaiah had stepped back from their growing friendship, hurting her. Nor had it helped that Isaiah had been the one to tell her about Lon.

She cut him a look. "I resented you at first, but you told me the truth and I should thank you for that. I just wasn't thinking clearly at the time."

"I know." His voice was husky.

"And then to find out about Dad cheating on Mom, and that we have another sibling out there we don't even know, made me think I could never trust again." She shrugged. "It all seems so trivial now with being abducted like this. Forced to lead these people through dangerous terrain, risking our lives for them. I don't know if we're going to live through this, Isaiah." She glanced up at him then, her lovely brown eyes that could coax anything out of him caressing his face.

Isaiah's heart floated. He shouldn't react to her this way, but how could he stop?

"These are big mountains," she continued. "We've made enough headway and we're far enough off our original path that I don't know how we'll ever be found."

"Your brother believes all we have to do is deliver these guys, and we'll be on our way. I hope it's that simple, but I don't see things happening that way." Isaiah wished he could take the words back. He needed to reassure her, not scare her more.

"We don't have much choice, except to hope that helicopters are searching for us already," she said, "but they have a lot of ground to cover before the next storm erases our tracks. So the coming hours, days, could be our last."

"Don't talk like that. You have to believe we'll be okay. You have to trust God. I know you do." Now listen to him, trying to convince her to trust God when Isaiah was struggling with that very issue. He believed they'd have to make their own way out of this. He wasn't even trusting God himself.

"You're right, I do. But people die every day."

She was right.

Leslie's face drifted across his mind. He hadn't known she was engaged at first. He'd fallen hard for her, and he'd thought she returned those sentiments. Then when he found out about Aaron, he'd thought he could change her mind. Why would she want to marry a man with anger issues? A man that would hurt her like that? When it became clear that she had every intention of going ahead with her wedding, and that Isaiah had only put more strain between her and her fiancé, he'd finally decided to back off. Should have done it much sooner. He'd gone to break things off for good, but he never got the chance. He'd been the one to find her body.

No matter how far he'd moved away, no matter how much distance he'd put between himself and his past, and how much effort he'd poured into starting a new life, those images would never leave him. His knees buckled and Isaiah caught himself, brushed the images aside. At least his past was nudging him to do the right thing now—tell Heidi while he had the chance.

"Heidi...I'm sorry for pulling away from you. Sorry if I hurt you." There was so much more to it. So much more he wanted to say.

She stared at him. "You didn't."

* * *

She'd lied.

The clouds resurfaced again and finally moved in, as though reinforcing her somber mood. Stomping along behind Isaiah as the snow fell thick and hard, wiping away their hope of someone spotting their tracks, Heidi couldn't get the look in his eyes out of her head. He'd hurt her all right, the moment he'd gone all nonchalant on her. She'd never forget that day, a defining moment in her life.

She wasn't sure when their relationship had started exactly, but she'd been sure when it ended, at least for her. Isaiah began giving her rides home after search and rescues. After work at the Avalanche Center they'd hang out together. Get dinner, or a soda, or catch a movie. Just friends, all along. Neither of them ever crossed that invisible line. But over time, they shared a few looks. Three years of that and Heidi's heart grew attached to Isaiah in ways she could never explain. His friendship meant the world to her, and his presence wrapped around her, protecting her and making her feel cherished.

Should a girl feel that way about a guy who was nothing more than a friend? They never talked about it, but she had a feeling he understood what she was thinking. She felt the attraction and suspected Isaiah did, too, but stepping over that line, becoming more than friends, would mean they'd risk losing what they had.

Maybe having more with Isaiah was worth the risk. And that's why that one evening while they waited on Cade and Leah to return from Seattle, she'd found herself looking into Isaiah's eyes and letting herself wish for more. Found herself wanting to trust him completely. She'd seen something similar in his eyes. Her heart had leaped at the possibility of freely loving him.

And her head had spun when the longing behind his gaze had shuttered closed, hiding his feelings from her. Everything about Isaiah had changed that day. His smiles weren't personal and special and just for her anymore. She could have been a stranger off the street, the way he treated her, though he was never unkind.

But he'd been scared that day. Apparently something more with Heidi hadn't been worth the risk to Isaiah, and yet his fear had shut down the friendship they shared anyway. He changed his work schedule so he no longer worked the same shift.

Nothing had been the same between them. After the hiking trip that ended with the loss of her friend, Heidi had needed Isaiah and he'd failed to be there for her. His choice. After that everything had spiraled downward and sent her into a darker place.

She couldn't stand to let Isaiah know that he'd held enough of a place in her heart to hurt her. But if he knew anything about her, he'd know she had lied. Still, her words had cut him all the same. She could see it in his eyes.

Her pain.

His pain.

But none of what she'd gone through compared to this nightmare. *Oh, Lord, please give us hope. Help us out of this somehow. Use us to show these people Your love and grace. Just... show up.*

The prayer lifted from her heart, but she'd never felt so alone. God was there. She knew He was, but why couldn't she feel Him? Get a sense of His presence?

What about all those verses in Psalm 139? She'd meditated on them, used them to help her get through her most painful moments, and yet here she was hiking through the wilderness and slipping back into the darkness.

She whispered to herself, "'If I say, "Surely the darkness will hide me and the light become night around me," even the darkness will not be dark to you; the night will shine like the day, for darkness is as light to you.'"

Where are You, God?

No answer.

But Heidi knew that her heart was too strung out. God's answer always came in the form of a still, small voice in her heart. And she always recognized His voice. No matter that the situation seemed hopeless, she would cling to Him the best she could.

And, as if He'd answered, the snow stopped falling, and the sky peeked through the dense clouds, if only a little. After her hurtful words to Isaiah, he'd left her behind, hiking on ahead, but he glanced back now and caught her gaze. He remained every bit the pillar to her that her brother was, and that made no sense.

Isaiah stopped.

He stood at attention and peered into the sky.

Heidi heard it, too.

A helicopter!

SAR had finally found them.

Oh, thank You, God!

The sound grew louder as the bird flew closer. Heidi couldn't contain her excitement. She searched the skies, waving her arms up and down. Jumping, too.

Something slammed into her, knocking her into the snow. Yanked her up by the arm. She gasped for breath.

Zach.

He dragged her, waving his gun around. If

Heidi could have managed it, she would have knocked it out of his hands. But his grip on her was too strong, and his brutality intimidated her. He'd had the exact opposite reaction to the sound of a rescue helicopter.

This helicopter would not be a friend to him.

"Run to the rocks and hide there or I swear I'll kill her!" He jammed the gun against her head and dragged her through the snow as if she weighed nothing.

Heidi only caught a glimpse of the terror on Isaiah's face, but they all ran for cover. No waving or catching the helicopter's attention. And the snow had covered most of their tracks from earlier. The mountains were beginning to eclipse the sun and whatever fresh tracks they'd made would likely go unnoticed from the air.

Running for her life through the deep snow, stumbling and falling, being snatched back up and dragged, Heidi felt her strength, her will-power melting. She operated on autopilot, keeping up with Zach and the others in order to survive. How had her life of saving and rescuing people twisted into this perverse experience that sucked the life from her?

If she made it back to Mountain Cove, life would never seem hard to her again. She would celebrate and be thankful. She would count even the smallest of blessings. She would connect with people she missed, she'd bridge the gap between her and Isaiah. Somehow. Someway.

They made it to the shadows of a spire that thrust high into the gray sky. The helicopter wouldn't fly nearly close enough to see them crouched behind where rocks sprung from the spire and other outcroppings, which had escaped being buried by snow and remained a dingy gray themselves. Only Heidi's bright fuchsia jacket could draw attention from the sky, and Zach had her tucked behind the rock to prevent discovery.

"Anyone make a wrong move and I'll kill you all." The words seethed from him, his hot breath a shock against her cold cheeks. How she hated feeling him this close to her.

Squeezing her eyes shut, she tried to calm her racing heart, slow her panicked breathing.

You are my Rock, God. You are my Rock, God.

The helicopter drew near. It was right there. If only they could jump out and wave. David had to be worried sick about them and must have contacted the Alaska State Troopers for a new search—one sent out for the search and rescue team themselves. Maybe they even knew about the armored-car-robbery fugitives. Knew what was going on. Then again, maybe they didn't have a clue.

Regardless, she, Cade and Isaiah were powerless to signal their would-be rescuers.

Zach had her pinned against the rock so hard, the gun pressed against her temple, she gasped for air.

Breathe in. Breathe out. An image of when Isaiah had said those words to her as this nightmare had only begun flashed in her thoughts. That seemed like an eternity ago. She opened her eyes.

Isaiah and Cade leaned against the rock opposite her, Isaiah's eyes locking with hers. In them, she saw the promise he'd made.

I'm here for you. I won't let anyone hurt you.

How she wanted to believe him. But right now, with Zach pressing his body over her, preventing her from signaling for help and rescue, Isaiah's promise fell flat.

It was dead to her.

ELEVEN

His gut twisted. The helicopter moved away, skirting the mountain in search of them.

He should have risked it. Should have fled the safety of cover and waved them down. So what if Zach shot him? That would be an even bigger mark against the guy. Didn't he know that? But Isaiah couldn't risk Heidi's life.

In fact, he was done watching Zach hurt her. He jumped to his feet, envisioning the instant he'd yank the man away and maybe take the gun from him, too. Cade held him back, but Isaiah shrugged free. It didn't matter.

Isaiah didn't have to get in Zach's face.

Jason beat him to it. He pulled Zach to his feet, the surprise clear on Zach's face.

"Why did you make us hide? That helicopter could have been our way out!" Jason's face grew even redder than it already was from the cold.

"What are you talking about?" Zach shoved

Jason. "We can't let them know where we are, or who we are. Can't let them see us."

Jason jabbed Zach's chest with his finger. "You said that no one would know who we are. No one would know where we're going. What makes you think the helicopter pilot would? Or was it all a lie?"

Rhea appeared confused by the whole thing, unsure which guy she should side with.

"Watch your mouth or I'll give you another bloody nose. I didn't lie to you. We just can't risk it. Even if the pilot didn't know, these guys would tell them."

"You could just hold them hostage, threaten to kill them and hijack the helicopter."

"Yeah, at least we'd be out of this frozen wilderness." Rhea added her opinion.

Zach's own people were ganging up on him. Isaiah shot a glance at Cade. Was this good or bad for them? The conflict would definitely grow worse as they continued their trek, and they would need to be prepared to take advantage of it, but only when the time was right.

Heidi had crawled away from Zach and stood up near a rock. Isaiah didn't think that Zach would see or care that he went to Heidi at the moment. Cade joined him, and took his sister in his arms. Isaiah had wanted to do that, but Cade had more right than he did.

"You okay?" Cade asked.

Her smile tenuous, she looked at Isaiah around Cade's shoulder. "Of course. How are you holding up?"

Cade released Heidi, and she stood there awkwardly, staring at Isaiah. Did she want him to hold her? No, he was reading her wrong. She'd made it abundantly clear, at least with her words, that she had no real feelings for him. And that was the way he wanted it. It was best for the both of them.

Then why was his heart pounding against his ribs, fighting for a way out?

He'd let her down, letting Zach manhandle her like that. But the man with the gun ruled them all, at least for now. The two men were still arguing, but Isaiah only cared about Heidi. She hung her head.

She was strong. Didn't need Isaiah to hold her together. But maybe he needed her. He was the one with trembling knees at the moment. He needed her to keep him strong. A pang zinged through him at the startling reality.

Isaiah ignored all the warnings inside his head and stepped forward, dragged her into his arms and held tight. *God, when will this be over?*

He wanted, oh how he wanted, to kiss the top of her head. To tell her how much he cared. But what would that accomplish in the midst of this chaos except to leave them both confused? So Isaiah said nothing at all. Just held on to Heidi, soaking up her goodness, willing her to know that next time he wouldn't let Zach get away with any of this.

That was another promise he couldn't keep. No, Isaiah wouldn't stand in Zach's way until he knew he could win without Cade or Heidi getting hurt.

Zach finally punched Jason, and they got into a scuffle on the snow-packed earth. Heidi and Isaiah parted to watch. Cade took a step forward. Maybe they could grab the guns.

On the other hand, maybe the weapons would go off and kill an innocent bystander. Before Cade or Isaiah could react, it was all over.

Zach hovered over Jason. "I don't care if you're my brother. Challenge me like that again and it will be the last time."

He crawled off the whimpering man.

His brother?

Now, that was news, though it made sense. Zach hadn't cared about Robbie, the man he'd shot back at the saddle. He hadn't mourned Liam's death, nor did he seem to care a lot about whether Rhea was around, but Jason—he cared about Jason, despite his threat.

And maybe they could use that fact against

Zach. Unless Zach cared more about the money, more about his survival than he did his own brother.

"Let's set up camp here. The rocks will protect us from the weather and it will be dark soon." Cade barked orders at them, his gaze landing on Isaiah.

Isaiah understood that Cade wanted to diffuse the tension to keep crazy Zach from shooting off his gun and his mouth again. They set up the tents, used the camping stove to melt snow for water and prepared the MREs. They'd run out of energy bars and would now be subjected to the food Isaiah detested. He'd hoped this would all be over before it came to that.

What's more, they were quickly running out of fuel. Zach stomped around the campsite with a scowl, and Rhea whimpered, afraid of the man she loved. Jason was in a rotten mood, too, leaning against the supplies and eating the last energy bar. He held a weapon now, charged with guarding his rescuers.

Heidi crawled into the tent she would share with Rhea, reminding Isaiah that he needed to figure out how he could protect her from a woman who wanted her dead. He hated to think of Heidi lying awake all night on guard for her life.

But with their captors at a distance and preoccupied, this was his chance to strategize with Cade. "What's the plan?" He kept his voice low, focused on melting snow for water.

Cade only grunted.

"Look, I know something has been eating you for weeks now. Just put that aside. We need to figure out our escape. Whatever reason you're mad at me can wait."

"I don't think that it can."

"What?" Surprised at his response, Isaiah poured melted snow into a cup and handed it to Cade.

"I see how you are with Heidi, so it can't wait."

Isaiah stiffened.

"I know about your past, Isaiah. I thought I knew you pretty well, considering the amount of time we spent together, but even then I always thought you were hiding something."

Isaiah sat back in the snow. "What do you know?" And he could guess how he'd found out. Had to be Leah, his legal-investigator wife, sticking her nose where it didn't belong.

"I know that you were a person of interest in a murder that was never solved. You changed your name and moved here to assume a new identity." Cade's look of betrayal filleted Isaiah.

Was Cade accusing him of the murder? If he felt that way, how could the guy even climb with Isaiah? How come he'd waited so long to confront him? "Please tell me you don't think I'm guilty."

Isaiah needed to hear that Cade trusted him.

"I don't want to think you're a murderer. No. I can't make myself believe that. So no, that's not it. It's that you hid all that from us, from me personally. You hid who you are. It's a trust thing with me. I thought I knew you, Isaiah. Thought I knew who you really are. But then I find out I didn't know you at all."

Isaiah absorbed Cade's words. He had expected to hear them at some point. He drew in a breath then dived in. "Cade, I meant no harm. You have to understand…"

Isaiah didn't say more. What could he say? The man had serious trust issues after learning of his father's infidelities. But Isaiah had to try. "Look, I'm innocent, but having people—a whole town of people—suspicious of you is like being guilty. I might as well have been guilty as far as they were concerned. So I wanted to start over. Is that so bad? I'm sorry that I didn't tell you sooner, but it wouldn't be much of a new life for me if I brought my past with me, would it? What if every time I looked at you, I saw that same suspicion in your eyes?" And in fact Isaiah had recognized it in Cade—he just hadn't wanted to believe it.

"Can't say that I would have done things any differently, but you're not the guy for Heidi so stay away from her."

Back when Isaiah and Heidi were growing close, when something was happening between them, Cade hadn't been happy about it. In fact, he'd been relieved when Isaiah had stepped away from Heidi. Maybe that was because of the secret he thought Isaiah carried, and now he knew the full of it.

As if Isaiah could stop caring about her here and now, especially in this situation. He'd really tried, but who was he kidding? He'd tried and failed miserably to not be seriously into Heidi Warren. Fortunately, that didn't matter—Heidi was definitely not into him, and he couldn't bear to break her heart after she heard about his past. Cade was sure to tell her if he hadn't already.

Isaiah couldn't look at the man. Resentment burned in his gut. "How did you find out?" He already knew, but wanted to hear it from Cade.

"Leah."

"I can't believe you had someone look into my background." Had Cade done it because he was worried about Heidi?

"It just…happened. A connection to another case she was investigating that took her all the way to Montana."

"I don't get it. Why now? Why did you wait until this moment to confront me?"

Cade exhaled long and hard. "I've trusted you in every way that counted, since we're on a SAR team. I tried to give you the benefit of the doubt that you had your reasons for keeping this a secret, and frankly, I just didn't know how to bring it up. I thought it was a moot point because you and Heidi weren't as close anymore, but this predicament seems to be pushing all those feelings to the surface. And seeing how you are with her, seeing that look in her eyes, has forced my hand."

Spoken like the overprotective father of a young girl. Did Cade even see that?

"I'm still the same Isaiah that you've known for almost four years now. Thanks for digging up the past I wanted to forget. Thanks for not trusting me." Isaiah stomped off into the darkness that edged their circle of light, feeling the isolation to his bones.

As soon as her tent was set up, Heidi crawled inside to rest on the sleeping bag. She was too tired to be hungry, and while she lay there, she could barely make out Cade and Isaiah talking. It didn't sound as if things were good between them. If only she wasn't so exhausted she might have edged closer to listen in on their conversation.

One thing she had heard clearly was Cade's warning to Isaiah to stay away from her.

Anger churned inside. She didn't need or want him to protect her. At least, not like that. Who did he think he was anyway? He wasn't her father. She could take care of herself. But he was her brother. Her heart softened a little. What kind of brother would he be if he didn't at least try to protect her?

She was capable of defending her heart from Isaiah. At least she thought she was, but all she could think about was the moment earlier—after the helicopter had come and gone, when Cade had finished hugging her. Isaiah had stood there, watching her. It was as if they'd both wanted to embrace each other, but each had held back for their own reasons. It had been kind of awkward and silly and so obvious. But Heidi had refused to give in to her crazy need for him.

That is, until she'd seen the longing and the desperation pouring from his gaze. All pretext washed away in the harsh reality of this dangerous adventure. Heidi almost had the sense that maybe it wasn't about Heidi needing him, but that Isaiah was the one in need.

Big strong Isaiah. Hard to grasp that he needed anything.

That image still dancing in her mind, Heidi

rolled on her back and stared at the tent ceiling in the growing darkness. She heard footsteps outside and saw the silhouette of a man passing between the tents.

Isaiah. He'd left the unpleasant conversation he'd had with Cade. She had a feeling it was about more than her. She allowed her thoughts to drift back to that moment when Isaiah had taken the step forward and grabbed her arms, tugged her to him. She'd gone willingly. And yes, she needed him, too. Not as a person who would watch her back on this journey, but as something much more. Something she couldn't even define, but she sensed its light in her soul growing bigger, kindling, instead of being snuffed out completely. With everything she'd been through, she thought that light had all but died.

She savored the memory of being in his arms for no other reason than just being there, and she'd allowed herself to soak him up. Frankly, she was too exhausted—both emotionally and physically—to keep fighting what she felt for Isaiah, even though he'd hurt her.

But something told her that he'd had his reasons. Good reasons. She'd never known Isaiah to do anything without thinking it through, and that was something she could take to the bank.

Ugh—the thought of the bank brought her

back to the robbery and their predicament and, oddly enough, at that moment Rhea crawled into the tent. Heidi didn't relish the prospect of trying to survive the night with Rhea. She'd likely have to stay awake to keep from being smothered or strangled in her sleep.

"You don't have to worry." Rhea tugged out her own weapon. "Zach gave me orders to watch you. Keep you from running away. He said I'd better not hurt you."

Heidi considered threatening Rhea with their little secret about the money. Then again, that might give Rhea more of a reason to kill her. "I'm too exhausted to go anywhere, aren't you? Besides, where would I go? Without the protection of the tent, I'd just die of hypothermia." Like Liam.

"Zach said you might run after the helicopter if it comes back."

Zach would be right. Heidi rolled over, putting her back to Rhea. She'd had enough of the woman. But maybe she'd give it one more try. "Rhea, remember that first night in the tent?"

"What of it?"

"Remember how you said you thought I was interested in someone?"

Rhea grunted.

"I thought you understood that I have no interest in your boyfriend. None. I thought we connected and had an understanding. You weren't going to tell my secret and I wouldn't tell yours." She thought they'd shared a common bond after their initial heart-to-heart, but Zach had destroyed that.

"I don't have a secret on you anymore. Everyone can see what's going on."

Heidi's pulse raced. She wanted to know what Rhea meant. Hear all the details about it as if they were silly schoolgirls, but she kept quiet. She'd tried to deny it for far too long and that must be why Cade had warned Isaiah away. He saw it, too. Heidi blew out a breath.

"So I got nothing on you. But don't worry, I won't kill you for it tonight."

"Thanks." Heidi didn't bother to hide her sarcasm. She had a few surprises for Rhea if the woman thought she could take Heidi out so easily.

TWELVE

The next morning they packed up the tents and prepared to hike on.

Before Cade led the group out, Isaiah held his gaze. "We're out of fuel."

"We'll be at the ice field in a few hours." Zach stepped close to Heidi.

Isaiah couldn't wait for that moment at the end of this ordeal when he would get some personal face time with Zach. He couldn't know for sure that he would get that chance, like the good guy did with the bad guy at the end of an action-adventure movie, but he could hope.

"We're not going to make it, sorry." Cade pulled on his pack. "At least not today. Not even by tonight."

"What are you talking about?" Zach ground out the words.

"Like Isaiah says, we're out of fuel, which means we don't have water. We'll get dehydrated. We need supplies."

"So we eat the snow."

"No. We have to melt the snow and heat the water or die of hypothermia," Isaiah said, catching Heidi's gaze.

She had that fire in her eyes as if she was about to knock Zach's nose into his brain. With Zach holding the weapon, Isaiah wasn't so sure now was the time, but any other time, he'd say, sure, go for it.

"What are you saying, exactly?" Jason inserted himself into the conversation, but with obvious caution. "Sounds like you know where we can get supplies."

Cade nodded. "There's an off-grid cabin just a few miles out of our way, but in the same general direction. A summer cabin, but maybe it will have items we could use. We should head there and stay tonight. Get what we need, then we can make it to your destination tomorrow, alive and well."

"It's a trick," Rhea said. "Zach, they're playing us. They're going to take us into an ambush."

"Shut up." Zach tucked his weapon way. "This isn't the Wild West."

His reaction confused Isaiah. "It's no trick," Isaiah said. "Without basic necessities our chances of surviving decrease exponentially. I don't think we'll make it otherwise."

A severe frown creasing his exhausted features, Zach studied Isaiah as though weighing whether or not to ignore their advice. "You don't *think*? There's a small window of time for me to make that rendezvous."

"You, Zach?" Rhea asked. "What about us? We're all going to be on that plane out, aren't we?"

"We, I meant to say we. How many times do I have to tell you to shut up?"

From the look on Rhea's face, it appeared Zach certainly wasn't good at keeping his friends. Isaiah wondered why she continued to take it. Unfortunately, they were all stuck following Zach for the moment.

"Zach, we're not going to meet the plane if we're dead." Jason kept his distance from his brother. "Call him up and tell him what's going on. Put him off a day. I don't want to die over money. Not even…" Jason caught himself before sharing the amount.

Zach probably thought Cade, Isaiah and Heidi wanted to steal the money and that knowing the amount would make it even more worth their while. Right. The only thing important to the three of them was their lives. Zach could have his money, no matter if it was a million dollars or more.

While Zach, Jason and Rhea argued over

risking the rendezvous point and stopping for supplies, Isaiah looked from Cade to Heidi. They each harbored their own brand of conflict with him, it would seem. But despite the tension between them, Isaiah hoped they could put their differences aside and work through this problem, which was quickly heading toward a fatal ending. Still, the future was unwritten. It could be changed.

Heidi gave an imperceptible nod, then Cade.

For years, they'd worked together on a SAR team, so they had that going for them. They knew each other well, and Isaiah knew then, they all shared the same thought—they had to make a move soon. The cabin would have to be it. But what would the move be? What could they do that wouldn't get one of them killed?

Though Isaiah didn't want to die anytime soon—he was only human, after all—he definitely wouldn't stand by and watch Cade or Heidi come to that end. Not while he had breath in him.

He'd racked his brain a thousand times to try to think of what he could have done differently, that is, besides not becoming involved with Leslie. Hindsight did him no good. What could he have done to save her? Too many questions with no answers, questions he couldn't afford to leave unanswered this time.

Zach was talking. Isaiah hadn't been listening.

"We're getting supplies at this cabin, but I don't think I need to remind you what's at stake if this is a trick. All you have to do to make it out alive is deliver us to the ice field and to our ride out. Don't try anything or I'll have to choose which one of you will live to lead us out. In case you're not any good at math, that means two of you will die in these mountains."

When Heidi spotted the cabin tucked behind a thick copse of evergreens, hope surged, and she picked up her steps. They all did. The trek through the mountains without any real shelter other than the tents had been long and arduous. No surprise there, but she'd always believed she was in top physical condition. Yet this experience challenged her beyond belief—and she was already stretched thin emotionally.

Maybe spiritually.

The snow wasn't as deep here, and they all hurried toward the cabin.

Isaiah got there first and appeared to jiggle the lock, Heidi wasn't sure. But he finally kicked the door in. Breaking and entering? But it was survival. Palpable relief poured from each of them as they filed into the dark, rudimentary cabin.

Cade got busy making a fire.

Isaiah found a kerosene lamp and lit it, then shone it around the cabin in search of supplies. Heidi wanted to follow but Zach closed in on Isaiah, maybe afraid Isaiah would come across a weapon of some kind.

While she helped Cade build a fire, she eyed the woodstove in the corner. Could they get that going, too? She could really use a cup of hot tea. Even coffee would do. Would it be possible they could find hot chocolate? She almost laughed at her racing thoughts. She was wishing for too much.

A frown under his brows, Cade was focused on his task.

"How did you know about this place?" she asked.

"Isaiah and I came across it while we were in the helicopter making our avalanche assessment rounds."

"Is it government property?"

"I don't know, but I doubt it would be stocked if it was. Likely private. Maybe even shouldn't be here."

Interesting. "How did you *know* it would be stocked?"

Cade glanced up at her. "I didn't. Still don't,

but a fire like this, the warmth of a cabin, of a roof over our heads for even one night is enough, isn't it?"

She nodded. "It is."

For the first time since this ordeal began, she started to think maybe they would survive, despite the odds—though Zach remained their greatest threat.

Jason whooped across the small cabin. "Food. It's like we hit the jackpot."

"Never thought I'd be excited to see a can of beans." Rhea pulled cans off the shelves, letting them fall to the floor.

Heidi blew out a breath. "You don't have to make a mess of things. This place doesn't belong to us."

"Hey, you're the one that broke in." Jason stumbled around the room.

The fire blazed, drawing everyone closer. Cade stood and faced the enemy. "I'm sure the owner wouldn't mind us using the cabin if it's a matter of survival. But we don't need to take advantage of or abuse his or her property. And I plan to repay them for anything we use, and include an explanation and a thank-you note."

"Aren't you thoughtful?" Zach ogled the canned food, uninterested in the debate.

"Can we get the woodstove going, too?" Heidi

asked. "Warm up some food. I see a water pump, so we might not need to heat snow for water."

"Already on it." Isaiah stepped out from the bedroom and started to work on the woodstove, a smile on his lips.

Heidi worked the pump, hoping she'd get water.

"Listen up." Zach raised his voice. "We are not here to get cozy and comfortable. We are here for those supplies, then we move on."

Rhea moaned. "I thought we agreed to stay tonight. Hike out tomorrow."

"I couldn't make contact."

"Well, try again," Jason said.

His own crew was ganging up on him again. Zach toyed with his weapon. Heidi wondered if he'd considered cleaning it while they were here. After their journey, the weapon might even malfunction. She'd watched Cade cleaning his weapons often enough, heard him talk about it. As for Heidi, she didn't like guns. Hadn't needed to use one with so many brothers packing.

Zach growled and frowned. He was losing control over his partners-in-crime and had to be exhausted, too. He left the warmth of the cabin to try to make contact with their ride on the SAT phone. Rhea and Jason followed, leaving Cade, Isaiah and Heidi all alone.

For a second, they stared at each other. "Should we make a run for it?" Heidi asked. "We could flee out the back. They wouldn't scc us. Wouldn't know until it was too late and they'd never find us."

"Don't kid yourself," Cade said. "We have no way to protect ourselves if they find us. They have their weapons *and* ours. Two of them are carrying, maybe three, though I haven't seen Rhea with one."

"I have." A pot of hot beans and what other real food she could find might keep them distracted longer. If only Heidi's mouth didn't water at the thought. She used a can opener she found in a drawer and opened several cans of beans, then poured them into a large pot. She searched the cabinets for salt, seasonings and spices.

"The risk is too high," Cade said. "I don't want anyone to get hurt."

"Three of us couldn't make it." At the stove, Heidi kept her voice low while she warmed the beans. "But one of us could break free. Go for help."

Oh, why had she said that? She couldn't stand the thought of losing either Cade or Isaiah. What if one of them escaped but didn't survive? Or what if Zach killed whoever stayed behind?

"Scratch that. I… We should all stay together. It's the only way."

"I think she's on to something." Isaiah spoke to Cade, didn't even look at her.

He was trying to cut her out of the decision. Heidi fumed, but kept her thoughts to herself. She knew they had little time, if they could even pull off an escape at all. The others would come back inside too soon. She swallowed the knot in her throat.

"Then it has to be her. She can be the one to get away."

The two men stared at each other long and hard. Heidi felt as if she wasn't even in the room.

"Guys, I'm here, right here. I need to be part of this conversation, and no, it's not going to be me. I wish I hadn't said anything." No way could she leave anyone behind.

Cade left the fireplace and stood behind Heidi. He turned her around. "I think Isaiah was right when he said that Zach isn't going to let us live once we get to the ice field. Why should he? We know who he is. It would be days, weeks, maybe even summer thaw before anyone found our bodies. The only way out is now. You have to leave. You have to be the one. We'll sneak some supplies into your pack and you go for help."

"But if I leave, then he'll kill you."

"No. He still needs a guide to the pickup point."

Isaiah stood too close. "You're burning the beans."

"Oh!" Heidi gasped. She removed them from the stove.

This time it was Isaiah who turned her to face him. "Your brother is right. Someone has to live. Someone has to call for help somehow. We'll cover for you."

"You're in the outhouse or something."

Heidi frowned.

"I have a better idea," Cade said. "Two of us go. Zach won't kill the one who stays behind, which will be me. I know my way around. I'm the only one who really knows how to get him there anyway," Cade said.

"Then why don't we all just leave now?" Heidi shook her head, hating their few options.

The cabin growing warm, Isaiah shrugged out of his coat. He scraped his hands through his hair. "I don't like any of this."

Her thoughts exactly.

"My idea is the strongest." Cade moved to the fire and warmed his hands. "But I hear voices outside and they're coming back in. We missed a chance to run, but we had to talk it through first. At least we had an opportunity. Let's agree on this. It's tonight or never."

"This evening, after they've eaten and they're tired, I'll take Heidi and we'll go for help." Isaiah slumped. "Are you sure about this, Cade?"

"It's the only way."

Like Heidi, Isaiah didn't appear convinced, but it was too late to discuss it further. Zach trudged inside, followed by his cohorts. His eyes grew wide when he saw the bowls of beans laid out for them. Heidi busied herself opening cans of tuna, as well.

"Who would think beans would ever look and smell so good?" Jason sat at the table and started eating as if he was famished.

"Did you reach your person?" Heidi asked. "I mean, are we staying tonight?"

"Why? Are you planning an escape?" Zach sneered.

"No." Heidi answered too quickly, she knew. Her pulse raced.

"Because let me be perfectly clear." Zach stepped closer. "Surviving the wilderness in tents while a blizzard is blasting away is one thing, but this cabin is much different. I'll need to tie you up tonight. If even one of you escapes, you'll hear the screams of whomever you left behind echo through the mountains."

Shaking, Heidi stared at the floor. She didn't

dare glance at either her brother or Isaiah. But Zach's threat rendered her helpless. It seemed strange that they were reduced to this…groveling to a maniac in order to survive.

THIRTEEN

Warmth from the fire suffused the cabin. Isaiah noticed everyone growing sleepy as exhaustion took hold, especially after filling their stomachs with the beans and tuna. If they made it out of this alive, he and Cade would make sure to replace all the group had taken from the cabin. Could be that the owner had left the supplies for just such an occasion.

Zach had not bothered to tie them up like he'd claimed, but Isaiah figured at some point he would get to that. Isaiah would do the same, if he were in Zach's position. Though in this warm and cozy cabin stocked with food, he and his gang seemed less intimidating than the dangers one could meet with if exposed to the elements outside, which made fleeing a less appealing option at the moment.

If they were bound, it would mean their chance of escaping according to their plan was dead. As he helped Heidi clean up the dishes in the small kitchen, only the dim light from the gas lamp and the fire across the cabin to illuminate their chore, he wondered what she was thinking.

Her lush chocolate mane fell forward, though slightly askew and tangled, and hid her face as she cleaned the bowls. Hiding her thoughts from him. As if he could read them if he could see her face—but there was a time, months ago, when he had felt that close to her.

The moment overwhelmed Isaiah.

The guard he'd put in place shifted. His resistance falling away, he surrendered and pulled her curtain of hair back, exposing her flushed cheek. Heidi slowly turned toward him and looked up, emotions he couldn't read pouring from her eyes. Well, one of the emotions he read well enough. Like a magnet it compelled him forward, tugged him closer, until his face was mere inches from hers. Her breath warm and soft against his skin, Isaiah did something he'd longed to do for months, maybe even since the moment he met her almost four years ago.

He covered her lips with his own, only the quiet and dim lighting protecting them from unwanted spectators. He felt her sweet and tender response, and beyond that, the flutter of confusing emotions that mirrored his own. Regret and loss mingled with longing, hopes and dreams.

Isaiah held passion and desire in a well-guarded dungeon. This wasn't the time or the place, but now that he'd done the forbidden and kissed her, he wanted to somehow convey that she was a precious treasure that he cherished. The fierce protectiveness he'd always harbored for her washed over him, even in this moment.

He cupped the silky skin of her cheeks, and her response nearly undid him. If only he could wrap his arms around her and unleash all his buried emotions, show her everything she meant to him.

The thought jarred him as if he'd fallen through a frozen lake.

Isaiah severed the connection, tugged away from her lips.

Heidi's eyes were soft at first, then widened when realization hit her, just like it had him. The rogue environment had washed away his guard. Made him weak and he'd given in to it.

"Heidi," he whispered, his voice throaty. He should apologize for taking advantage of her and the situation. But he couldn't apologize for that kiss. Why hadn't he kissed her long before this? If he had, maybe everything would have been different between them. And now this moment had been their first kiss, shared at the worst possible time and place, under the watchful eyes of criminals and killers.

What did that say about Isaiah and Heidi's relationship? Did it mean that nothing else could ever break them apart, should they choose to build something between them? Or did it mean they were doomed to fail from the start?

By the fire, Jason struck up a conversation with Cade. Jason's words pulled Isaiah completely back into reality. Something about looking for rope to tie them up for the night. Isaiah wouldn't bother helping him. All Jason had to do was dig around in the mountain-climbing-gear packs.

Isaiah and Heidi continued with their chore, as though the kiss had never happened.

Had Cade seen them? Had anyone else noticed? Maybe they were all too overwhelmed with their own worries.

Once again their predicament weighed on Isaiah and he realized he wasn't thinking clearly. He shouldn't have kissed her, after all, letting his deepest feelings for her surface. His weakness appalled him. He shouldn't have any feelings for her. None. Even if he allowed himself to love again, he didn't deserve her.

Heidi reached for a dish, her fingers brushing his, then reached over and covered his hand with her own. She didn't look at him, just kept her head down, but her action conveyed more to him than he could have asked for. The kiss was much more than a moment of weakness for her. She spoke to him in a silent language that sent his heart and mind scrambling to find traction. Maybe he'd been wrong to think that keeping his past a secret was the only way to move on with his life. In order to move on, he had to open up and tell all. Cade and Leah already knew the truth, but Heidi was the most important person in Isaiah's life. He'd admit that much.

And maybe he needed to reveal his past to her.

She glanced up at him, a soft smile inching across her face, and he knew...he *knew* that once he told her—with everything she'd been through—she would be lost to him forever.

Heidi worked to put the dishes back, tucking them into the cabinet nice and neat, doing the best she could to respect the owner's property. She'd also picked up the cans Rhea and Zach had thrown on the floor haphazardly when searching the pantry. Acid burned her insides at their disregard for others, but she shouldn't be surprised, considering they had abducted a search and rescue team and forced them to guide them through the mountains.

The last bowl clinked and, before she closed the cabinet door, Isaiah's face filled her vision.

"Heidi." The way he said her name, the same

husky way he'd said it moments before, after he'd kissed her, crawled all over her. She could live on that sound for months.

She thought her trust in love and happily-ever-after's had been tarnished for good—destroyed, more like. But Isaiah made her want to believe in good things again. Was he the right man? Could he make her believe in the possibility of a lasting love? Heidi sucked in a breath. How could she possibly think about a future with Isaiah when they were in survival mode?

"Are we still on for tonight?" he asked, keeping his voice almost too low for her to hear.

His question confirmed she needed to focus back on their reality. She shook her head and whispered, "They're looking for rope. We can't escape."

"I think I can get us out of it."

Another, more vigorous shake of her head. "Didn't you hear Zach's warning?"

"He won't harm Cade. He's his only way out."

"Maybe not right away, but eventually he would."

"That will be all our fates, Heidi, if we don't go for help. This is our chance."

"No. I can't leave my brother alone with the guy who is going to hurt him. We just have to trust God for another way out." *Where are*

You, God? Her heart sent up the silent prayer once again.

Isaiah's gaze held hers, the disappointment in his eyes running deep, but mixed with fear and concern for her safety. Fear for his closest friend, her brother Cade. She knew he cared about Cade but both of them were basing this nonsensical plan on protecting Heidi, and she wouldn't have either of them risking themselves on her account. There had to be another way.

"The three of us should stick together. I wish I had never said anything."

It had been her initial idea, after all.

"Then we can all go. We'll all escape together," Isaiah suggested.

"Talking Cade into this won't be that easy, but that's the only way I'll go."

It would increase the chance of Zach following them, but how far could the guy make it without their help?

The seconds ticked by slowly with Isaiah standing far too close. Heidi could hardly breathe. For the longest time she'd known her feelings for this man ran long and deep. Any woman would find him attractive with his broad shoulders and strong, trim physique. Thick hair she wanted to run her fingers through. Deep, penetrating gaze that could see right through her. She'd been caught up in all that was Isaiah at some point, no doubt there. But it was more than that now.

The guy knew how to listen, really listen. She'd never met a guy like that. Or maybe it was just the way his eyes watched as though he lived on every word she said. But he was easy to talk to. All that had changed between them when he'd pushed her away. Not so much with words but with actions, and because he'd stopped looking at her with that penetrating look.

For a while Heidi had thought he couldn't look at her because he cared too much and didn't want her to know it. Or at least she'd lied to herself, convincing herself that was the reason. She couldn't bear to think of it any other way because it was much too painful to think that Isaiah would willingly push her away. That he didn't want her anymore—though they'd never before crossed the lines of friendship, not until moments ago when he kissed her, giving her what she'd dreamed about all those months ago.

But why here? Why now? Heidi thought she might know. Somewhere deep inside, the fear that their lives were coming to an end wouldn't leave her. Maybe Isaiah sensed it, too, and wanted to show her what he hadn't been able to reveal before.

She closed the cabinet, pulling them both out of their imagined private moment, hidden away behind an open door. Heidi wasn't sure why Isaiah had pushed her away in the past.

But that didn't matter because she had reasons of her own to keep her heart far and away from Isaiah or any man. Her head ached. She regretted that kiss, but her heart would never ever forget it. Still, she'd do well to remember the reasons she must try to forget Isaiah and his kiss—even though by tomorrow evening that all might not matter. They could all be dead and buried beneath a field of ice.

FOURTEEN

Isaiah watched Jason tie Cade's hands and feet to a chair. He huffed. If Cade wanted out of that, he could easily break the old rickety chair apart and be done with it. Instead the guy went along with these miscreants like he had no other choice.

Isaiah grew tired of playing this game. They had choices, all right. They could take control of this situation. Should have done it long ago. With Zach and Jason showing severe signs of exhaustion, now would be the perfect time to gain the upper hand. Maybe that's what Isaiah had been counting on all along—that he could outlast these rookies.

Unfortunately, Cade's eyes slid to Isaiah as if he could read his mind. His frown and narrowed gaze were a warning to Isaiah. They knew each other too well. Isaiah had never imagined himself in this situation. Of course, who would? But he never thought he'd be this torn about what to do. He'd never been so indecisive in his life except, well, where Heidi was concerned. But he slammed the door on those thoughts. Nothing mattered except surviving this ordeal.

Even if he managed to break free from the rope and untie Heidi as well, she would likely refuse to go with him as they had planned. Apparently, they still hadn't agreed on what to do, especially after Zach's threats.

There were trees here, plenty of cover if they ran this time. It wasn't as if they would be running across the snow—easy targets for Zach to shoot at—which had been the terrain for their entire trek until the cabin.

But the thought of Cade or Heidi taking a bullet rocked him. Should they try to escape or not?

God, what is the right thing to do?

Silence.

Not knowing the answer drove him up the wall.

But Isaiah did know one thing: even Cade had finally realized that their fates were sealed if they didn't find a way out. And Isaiah couldn't take the kowtowing anymore, not when he and Cade were both far stronger than their male captors. All they needed was to grab the weapons.

All Isaiah needed was a chance.

God, just give me a chance.

He eyed the situation. Zach looking on as

Jason did all the dirty work. He didn't see Rhea. She must have been exploring the other room in the cabin. Jason finished tying the knots on Cade's ankles. He'd laid his weapon over on the hearth, easy enough for Isaiah to reach. Zach played around with his gun as usual, but leaned back in his chair like a kid.

Once Jason tied Isaiah up his chance would be gone.

He kicked the leg of Zach's chair and it fell back. Isaiah knocked the gun from his grasp, then reached for Jason's weapon on the hearth just as Jason clued in and lunged for the gun. From the chair where he was bound, Cade leaned over and onto Jason, doing at least that much to help.

Isaiah had the weapon. He motioned for Jason and Zach to stand against the wall.

"Heidi, get Zach's gun. Then untie Cade. We need to make a call on Zach's SAT phone. Call for help. Get the Alaska State Troopers here." He didn't want to guard these guys any longer than he had to. In fact, he considered just leaving the three criminals here. It wasn't as if they could make it through the mountains themselves. They would be trapped until someone came for them. A SAR team backed up by Alaska State Troopers this time. "And then we're getting out of here. We're taking all the camping gear and the weapons with us."

Heidi's eyes grew wide and she lunged toward Isaiah. She didn't agree with him? "Watch out, Isaiah!"

Pain sliced through his head. Darkness edged his vision.

Shards of a vase tumbled down his shoulders and hit the floor. Isaiah fired the gun into the ceiling to gain control, but Zach and Jason tackled him to the ground. Behind them, he saw Rhea.

She'd been the one to take him down.

"I'm going to kill you." Zach flashed a knife in Isaiah's face. Isaiah believed him. The man had done it before to one of his own.

Isaiah had been an idiot, but he'd been desperate.

"No. Please don't, Zach." Heidi sounded more desperate than Isaiah.

He didn't want her begging for his life, putting her own in danger. Why hadn't he paid more attention to Rhea? He hadn't really considered her a threat. Jason kicked Isaiah in the kidney and pain erupted.

Zach stood up, getting off Isaiah and letting him breathe. "Did I tell you to kick him?" He stared his brother down.

Come on, Jason. Stand up to the guy for once.

Heidi was suddenly next to Isaiah, her face in his. "Are you okay?"

"You mean other than being an idiot?"

She smiled, the kind of pained smile that came from a situation like this. Zach yanked her away. Isaiah tried to stand but Jason shoved him back down with his booted foot.

"Get your hands off me." Heidi twisted from his grasp. "The only way you'll make it to the ice field is with our help. Haven't you noticed it takes all of us to help you rappel the cliffs, guide you and set up the tents? You'd better not lay a finger on him, or you can forget about going anywhere."

Zach just stared at her. So did Isaiah. Really? Heidi had blown up in his face. He'd never seen her do that. He wanted to cheer her on, but this was a nasty situation. She'd just faced off with a killer.

Zach smirked, a lascivious grin of the worst kind. "I like your spirit. You've got real fight in you. I haven't seen that in a woman in a long time."

Isaiah caught Rhea stiffen at those words. That did not bode well for Heidi. Only put her back in the crosshairs of Rhea's imaginary sniper rifle. Or maybe even a real gun.

Heidi stiffened and took a step back. Drawing Zach's attention to her hadn't been a good play, but she'd done that to protect Isaiah. He found himself the reason someone was in danger. Again.

Wanting to stand and protect Heidi, he shoved Jason's boot away and stood, dizziness making the room tilt. This was all his fault, after all. He'd gambled with their lives and lost.

Zach inched closer to Heidi. "I like you. So this time, I'll let your friend live. But I have to hurt him."

Isaiah didn't have time to think about what those words meant. Stabbing pain in his head rendered him helpless just before darkness took him.

Her wrists and ankles bound, Heidi lay on the floor on a sleeping bag near the fire. Tears flowed freely and she wished she could wipe the salty moisture that stung her cold-reddened cheeks away.

Unconscious, Isaiah rested against the wall on the other side of the room without a blanket. His hands and feet were tied as well, and blood oozed from a gash on the back of his head. Another one. She couldn't stand to see him like that—big, brave Isaiah incapacitated. Hurt. She wanted to go to him and patch up his wounds. Make sure he was okay.

He'd tried. She'd give him that. It was more

than either she or Cade had done. He'd wanted
to escape and maybe if she had agreed to go,
they would all be in a different situation.

"Don't cry, Heidi," her brother whispered.

He was still propped up in the chair. An un-
comfortable way to sleep. But they weren't in a
position to make demands after what had happened. They were happy to let Zach and the
others sleep in the bedroom. There wasn't any
chance of escape with Isaiah incapacitated.

"Why is this happening?" Heidi kept her
voice low. "Why can't we get away?"

"I'm sorry that I let you down. I just thought
if we saw this through, we'd be better off than
taking any risks by trying to overpower them.
I admit I made a mistake."

"It's not your fault, Cade. You're probably
right. Isaiah tried tonight and see what happened? Zach was going to kill him."

"You saved him. But I can assure you he
wouldn't want you to put yourself at risk. And
I don't want you to risk your life for either of
us. We're big boys and can take care of ourselves. So if it comes to that, don't try to save
me. Understand?"

Heidi shook her head. No, she didn't understand. She could take care of herself, too, and
was tired of being overprotected all the time.
So what if Zach liked Heidi and she'd used that

to persuade him not to harm Isaiah? Though, she knew she'd better watch out for Rhea. She didn't doubt the woman might try to shove her off a cliff again, simply because Zach had paid her a compliment.

"And Isaiah…he isn't the guy for you."

Where had that come from? Heidi struggled to find a response.

"When we get out of this, and we will, just keep your distance. You don't really know him."

"What?" Why was Cade saying this? The words wounded her. Isaiah wasn't awake to defend himself.

"He isn't who you think."

"Just shut up, okay? This isn't the time." She didn't want to hear Cade saying negative things about the man she'd kissed earlier. About a man he called his friend. Cade only stirred the tumult inside her heart all over again.

Isaiah groaned. Had he heard Cade's negative words?

Heidi could protect herself. And she could protect her own heart, thank you very much. She wasn't afraid of Isaiah or whoever Cade thought he really was.

Another groan and mumble from Isaiah was all it took to have Heidi squirming in her restraints.

"Help," Heidi called. "Somebody untie me. I need to help Isaiah."

She'd admit that Zach's reaction to her had given her a measure of courage she wouldn't have otherwise felt.

"Heidi, no," Cade hissed under his breath.

He might be her older brother but he couldn't control her. She could make her own decisions.

"Hello, anybody?"

"What's the racket in there?" Jason called from the bedroom.

"I need you to untie me," Heidi yelled.

Jason lumbered into the living room, the firelight barely illuminating his lumpy hair and worn face. "What's the problem?"

"Untie me, please. Isaiah's hurt. I need to make sure he's okay."

He rolled his head back, turned around and walked from the room.

"Hey!" Heidi's call was loud and sharp. Zach had to have heard that time. A tremor of fear rolled through her. Was she making a mistake? Would she only cause Isaiah more harm?

Jason turned, a scowl spreading over his face. She had to try another tactic.

"You want to make it to your rendezvous, don't you?"

He straightened.

"Then I need to make sure Isaiah is going to be well enough to help us tomorrow. We have to make good time, do you understand?" Now she sounded as if she was talking to a child. But maybe that's what it took to get it through Jason's thick skull. Anyone who would follow a person like Zach around, even if it was his brother, had to be a little dense.

Scratching his head, he nodded. "I suppose you're right. But try anything and I'll kill both of you before Zach can intervene. Don't think I won't."

Heidi wasn't sure, but she had a feeling Jason wasn't a killer. Just his brother. But now that she thought things through, maybe Zach had only shot his buddy after he was already dead to scare the SAR team. But did any of that really matter? It wasn't as if she could count on her theory.

After Jason untied her, she crawled over to Isaiah. "Can you get me a first aid kit? There's got to be one in the cabin somewhere."

She wished Zach would have let her take care of Isaiah from the beginning, but she and Cade had been duly terrified, and didn't want to push the man into killing Isaiah, or either of them for that matter. Jason returned with the kit and Heidi made fast work of cleaning the lacerations beneath Isaiah's thick head of hair. She bandaged where needed, wishing she had an ice pack for the knot.

Rolling him gently onto his back, she was

surprised to see his lids blink, then slide open. His hazel eyes stared back.

"Are you okay?" she asked.

A weak grin split his lips. "I am now."

FIFTEEN

They left the cabin at first light and lumbered through the snow-laced woods, wearing their regular boots this time. No snowshoes required, since the snow was packed. The most expeditious route to the ice field meant hiking over an intermediate peak, though Isaiah might refer to it as more of a swell. They'd made it over, but were now hiking down a steep slope into a slim gorge.

If Isaiah remembered this region correctly, the gorge should widen into a lake where they would find the glacier that would lead them to the ice field. He ignored the sledgehammer pounding his head. Probably had a concussion, but who cared. They were already in a death trap, so a concussion was a small price to pay for his lame attempt at an escape. At least they had all gotten plenty of sleep, food and water, and for whatever it was worth, were reenergized.

To a degree.

Today they were on the last leg of this nightmarish trek. He hoped this experience wouldn't forever scar the way he looked at the mountains. Only God could create such splendor.

Dizziness threw him off balance. At the wrong moment, that could be deadly. Isaiah leaned against the iced-over rocky wall that morphed from the slope, grappling for traction.

Heidi called out from behind him, too far away to be of any help. Zach had him isolated, hiking alone. None of them would be close enough to strategize an escape again. Their job was simple. If they kept at this pace, they would make it by late afternoon, just in time for his rescheduled rendezvous.

Isaiah couldn't stand the thought of Zach getting away. And Zach probably couldn't stand the thought of anyone identifying them or telling their strange story. Zach would not allow them to live, even Heidi whom he liked. He couldn't afford to keep them alive. But there was no sense in Isaiah rehashing what he already knew. Maybe deep in his subconscious he was looking for the remote chance, the possibility of a reason to hope that Zach would let them live.

Isaiah's failed attempt at freedom last night churned in his gut, adding to his painful headache. The blinding white expanse of snow only made the pain worse. He should never wish for clouds or a storm, but he prayed for one right now. And he would take the risk they'd been unwilling to take earlier and flee with Cade and Heidi into the elements. Dying at the hands of their captors couldn't be their fate. Somehow they would survive. They had to.

God, I feel so weak now. I've failed too many times. Help me to not fail this time. Please be strong where I am weak. Maybe I acted last night without praying first, and I'm sorry, but make a way for us. Help me protect Heidi. If she dies, if I don't do enough, I don't know how I can live with that.

Isaiah trailed along next to the snow-patched granite edging their hike down the slope, though it really wasn't a slope anymore. It was a rocky ledge allowing them access to lower elevations, but also providing a quick suicide jump for anyone who so desired one.

Pebbles mixed with snow trickled from somewhere above.

Uh-oh.

He pressed himself flat against the wall. Looked behind him at Heidi and Zach, who followed his lead.

Rhea was closer to Cade up at the front of the line this time. Something rumbled above. More pebbles, rocks and bigger boulders poured down. On top of that, a rush of snow piled high. A rock slide.

Isaiah couldn't see Cade. Heidi was at Isaiah's side, trying to push past, but Zach pulled her back.

"Cade!" Her scream echoed in his ears, in the mountains.

Isaiah held tight, stopping her from rushing forward. Not yet.

"It's not safe. Wait until we're sure it's over."

"Let me go!" She tugged.

Isaiah released his grip. Who was he to control her? She moved past him.

But he'd try with words anyway. "Heidi... please, wait."

She paused and glanced back at him, dread pouring from her eyes.

"Let me check on them," Isaiah said.

Heidi covered her face and nodded, sobs racking her body.

He didn't blame her for a moment of weakness. It was a hard thing to see someone you loved mangled, bloodied. A memory iced over him. He shook it off. Creeping forward, Isaiah gave a wide berth to the pile of rocks and snow in case more followed.

His heart hammered at the thought of what he might find. He hoped that Cade wasn't caught beneath the rubble somehow. Even if he were alive, Zach would kill him now, finish the job.

"Over here," Cade called.

Hearing Cade, adrenaline galvanized Isaiah and he carefully maneuvered a slim path between the drop-off and the debris. On the other side of the massive pile, Cade stood next to the rocks, removing them, tossing them aside. He glanced up at Isaiah. "It's Rhea. Help me."

Fear and pain streamed from Rhea's golden eyes as she looked up from where a boulder had pinned her legs—crushed, more like. *Oh, Lord, help us.* This was not good. Not good at all. He never wanted to see anyone injured or in pain, even if that person had made the wrong choices. Everyone had made a bad decision at some point in their lives. Hers had simply been to fall for the wrong person. Not as if he couldn't relate to that.

He dropped to his knees to brush the smaller rocks and rubble away from her body. "I'm so sorry. Just stay calm. We're going to get you out."

Then Zach appeared. "Rhea..."

His voice conveyed everything. His disappointment that she'd been hurt. That she was pinned. His resignation that she wouldn't be making the rest of the journey with him.

The sound was heart-wrenching.

Zach fell to his knees, too, next to Isaiah. "Rhea, how did it happen? Did Cade push you?"

Surprise registered in her eyes, and for a moment, Isaiah wondered if she would lie and blame someone else for her misfortune. But Rhea had been reduced to a person who depended on others for her life, and she knew Zach well enough to know she couldn't count on him to defend her or help her. The SAR team was her only hope now.

"No, no. Cade is helping me to get out. I'm going to be fine." Desperate, she lied to herself now.

"You're not going to be fine," Zach said. "I don't have time to wait for these guys to dig you out. And then what? I'm supposed to carry you? Your legs are crushed. You're going to…"

Die.

He was about to say it, but even Zach had enough human decency in him he didn't want to throw another stone on Rhea.

"She'll be all right. We're digging her out," Cade said. "I'll carry her. Do you hear me?"

Isaiah and Cade tossed rocks. Heidi, too. The boulder crushing her legs was the one to worry about, and Isaiah wasn't all that certain that removing it without the prospect of immediate medical attention was a good idea. She could bleed out, depending on the damage. They weren't prepared to treat such a traumatic injury.

Lord, please show us what to do. How do we save her?

Zach leaned in and kissed Rhea long and hard. Isaiah recognized it for what it was.

A goodbye kiss. The brute. So much for his sense of decency.

"If you love me, you'll let me go. Isn't that how the saying goes? If I don't leave now, then I'll miss my rendezvous. You know you're not going to make it anyway. Do you love me, Rhea?"

"How can you be so cruel?" Tears rushed from Heidi's eyes. The compassion she felt for Rhea, a woman who wanted to kill her, moved Isaiah to the core. "You are a sick, brutal creature. You're not even human!"

Zach stood and gathered the gear he carried. "You can't save her," he said to Cade. "We need to go."

Cade didn't stop digging the rubble away from Rhea. Isaiah and Heidi kept digging as well, wanting to save her, yet realizing how futile their efforts were.

Zach tugged his weapon out and aimed it at the injured woman. "Let's get moving. We don't have time to dig her out and she's going to die anyway."

Rhea moaned and whimpered from her pain, and the sheer terror of watching the man she loved, the man she'd followed, prepare to kill her.

Isaiah, Cade and Heidi stepped in front of Rhea to prevent Zach from shooting. "No!"

"I'm not leaving without her," Cade said.

"Have it your way." Zach pointed the weapon at Cade's head.

Heidi thrust herself in the path the bullet would take, breathless desperation emanating from her. "Please, Zach. Cade isn't a threat to you. Let him stay to comfort Rhea. Help her if he can. Maybe they can even catch up."

The determination behind Zach's eyes relaxed into indecision. He definitely had a soft spot for Heidi. Maybe Zach was even a little glad Rhea wouldn't stand in his way now. That tore at Isaiah's insides. He couldn't stand for that insane murderer to look at Heidi that way. But his protests would only put her in more danger.

"We all know they're not going to catch up to us. I should put them out of their misery now."

Time for Isaiah to step up. "Save your bullets and leave them here. They'll die from the elements anyway. Hypothermia, another storm. But you never know when you'll need your ammunition. A rogue bear. Something." Convincing Zach they were as good as dead anyway was the only way to save Cade and Rhea. He hoped Heidi understood this.

He shared a knowing look with Cade. God willing, he would survive and get them help. Cade's eyes urged Isaiah to take care of his sister. Protect her. Odd, considering he'd warned Isaiah to stay away earlier, but Cade had been reduced to raw survival instincts, just as they all had. Cade would stay behind to help Rhea and entrusted Isaiah to protect Heidi.

Isaiah used that knowledge to steel himself when Heidi suddenly refused to leave Cade's side. Cade hugged her, then gripped her shoulders, whispering something only she could hear, then he looked to Isaiah for help.

But it was Zach who yanked her away. "We have to go, sweetheart."

She ripped from his grip and rushed back to Cade. Isaiah thought she'd lost her mind. She'd been the one to suggest he stay with Rhea to begin with, but that was out of necessity. Now the realization that this could be the last time she saw her brother caved in on her. It caved in on Isaiah, too. He tore his gaze away and worked up the courage to do what he had to do.

Drawing in a deep, ragged breath, he wrapped his arm around Heidi and hauled her away from Cade, practically carrying her as she kicked and screamed. She'd hate him for this, and might never forgive him.

Heidi screamed Cade's name, an ear-shattering, gut-wrenching sound. Isaiah questioned if he was even doing the right thing, and the resulting anguish nearly crushed him.

When she finally calmed down, resigned to Cade's fate, he released her. She shoved away, unwilling to look at him. Now it was up to Isaiah and Heidi to lead the way, but it appeared she wanted no part of sharing the task with him. As he hiked forward into the widening gorge, he realized something—carrying Heidi, the chaos that ensued after Rhea's accident, had prevented him from grabbing his backpack and the other gear. Had prevented Zach from noticing.

That meant that a pack with supplies and a tent had been left behind for Cade. Isaiah glanced over his shoulder at Heidi. Still brooding. He doubted she was putting on a show to intentionally keep Zach from noticing the pack.

All the same, Cade had what he would need to survive.

Thank You, Lord.

Despair hovered over Heidi, a dark cloud blocking the blinding white of the snow— maybe not from her eyes, but certainly from her thoughts. And her heart.

Rhea gone.

Cade gone.

Persuading Zach to let them live seemed the only answer, but then what? How would they survive the night when the temperatures dropped? Clouds hedging the mountains to the west told her another storm chased them. Nothing new. Nothing surprising. The Coast Range of southeast Alaska was one of the most inclement places on earth.

Frankly, she was surprised they had survived this long. Heidi fought the dismal feelings snowing heavily down on her, burying her deep. Smothering her. It was all she could do to simply shove one boot in front of the other and trudge on. At some point, the terrain had changed and Isaiah had made them don their crampons, but she couldn't remember when.

She still reeled from Cade choosing to stay with Rhea, who would likely die within the next few hours from her injuries. Her big, brave brother—always looking for a way to help and serve. To do what was right when he had the ability to do so. That had been his mantra, ever since Grandma Katy had hung up the cross-stitch that displayed it. What would Grandma think today, if she knew that Cade had given his life to keep that scripture alive and true in him?

And Leah. Poor Leah! A whimpering groan

escaped Heidi and she stumbled. Cade didn't even know yet, but Leah had purchased a pregnancy test the very night they'd started on this rescue mission. Heidi came across Leah at the drugstore, asking the pharmacist about the ones kept behind the counter. So much for privacy in a small town.

But why, oh why, didn't Cade put Leah, his own wife, above Rhea—a woman who'd given her life to following a criminal and murderer? A woman who had wanted to kill Heidi.

Zach grabbed Heidi's arm to assist her. "Hey, sweetheart. Too bad about Rhea and your brother."

As if he cared. She wouldn't respond to him. Wouldn't say a word, though a million accusations blasted through her mind. If she opened that gate, she might never get it closed again, and the force of her words might crush Zach. On the other hand, maybe she should lay into him after all. But it was his reaction she feared.

Zach leaned in closer. Jason walked on the other side of her. Isaiah was up ahead. She was furious with him. Couldn't stand to look at him, even though she understood his actions. She hadn't tried hard enough to save her brother, either.

"Get away from me." She freed her arm from Zach and pushed ahead of him.

He caught up. "I hated to lose Rhea. She was a good woman. But now that she's out of the picture—"

Oh, that was it. "Are you insane?" Heidi stopped now, spitting mad. "I could never ever be interested in a murderous, backstabbing—"

"Hey! Look up ahead!" Isaiah's shout drew everyone's attention to him.

Zach and Jason all but forgot about Heidi and scrambled to meet Isaiah. They left her gasping for breath, to suffer in her own misery. She gazed behind her. How far was it again to Cade and Rhea? Could she simply leave now and take tents and supplies to them?

"Heidi." Isaiah was next to her then. "Come see, we're near the glacier that will take us to the ice field. It will still take us hours we probably don't have, but we have to try."

The pain in his eyes raw, she knew she'd tortured him, helped to drive in the nails of guilt even deeper.

"I don't care about that. I only care about getting back to Cade." She realized then that Isaiah had given Zach and Jason a distraction before Heidi lost complete control.

She wanted to thank him for that, but the image of Isaiah hauling her away and holding her against her will, her screaming and clawing, played across her mind. She had no words for him. The whole thing was an awful picture she would never forget.

But something was missing in that picture. What was it?

Her chest squeezed. "Isaiah, your pack with supplies. The tent."

A half grin slid onto his cheek and he nodded. He didn't have to say more because that was all Heidi needed to know. Cade would survive, and maybe, if he could get them help, Rhea, too.

But even more important—she had cried out to God, asking where He was.

And now she knew. He was here. Watching over them. Guiding them. And she also knew that while she'd been struggling with her faith, Isaiah had been praying every step of the way.

There wasn't anything she wanted to do more at that moment than step into Isaiah's arms. But with Zach's state of mind now about Rhea being out of the way, Heidi couldn't let her feelings for Isaiah show, or Zach would quickly dispense with him. They were near enough to the ice field that Zach might believe he could make it there on his own.

"We have to make sure Zach understands about the dangers of crossing the glacier and the ice field. About the danger of falling into a crevasse. We still have miles to go. He still needs us." She hated the knot in her throat.

Isaiah touched her chin. "Don't worry. We're going to make it."

But he had forgotten how well she knew him. How easily she read him, and his eyes told a much different story.

SIXTEEN

Isaiah saw hope flicker to life in Heidi's eyes. She would be okay, but for a while there he'd been worried, seriously worried, about her state of mind. They had to see this through to the end, whatever that meant. Isaiah had to keep praying, too. He couldn't stop. This was a battle in all senses: physical, emotional, mental and spiritual.

Heidi had to stay focused. Keep it together. And for his part, all Isaiah had to do was keep her alive until they were rescued, or he and Heidi could escape. He was afraid for Cade as well, but that was completely out of his hands. Cade had a better chance of survival than he and Heidi at this point. Cade wasn't facing a bullet from Zach anymore. He had a chance to get away and flag down the searchers. At least the helicopter had given them confirmation that a search for them was already under way.

God, please let them find us in time. Help me

to keep Heidi safe and alive. Help Cade and Rhea, too.

They approached the moat, or the wall that signaled the start of the glacier, which towered above them. Isaiah looked over at Heidi, who watched him, gauging his reaction. With everything that had happened, he'd pushed this moment to the side.

He blew out a breath. By their expressions, even Zach and Jason seemed to understand the enormous task ahead of them. At least Heidi had made sure they had enough crampons for everyone before they even began this ordeal. Without them he wasn't sure they could have tackled the glacier.

But that was the only positive. How did Isaiah tell Zach that there was simply no way they could cross the glacier and make the ice field in time for his rendezvous after this big push? How long would it take for Zach to realize that on his own? And then when he did, what would happen next?

He wished one of the glacier tour guides was here with them. Those guys spent plenty of summers guiding visitors on such terrain and knew everything there was to know. Isaiah, not so much. He preferred to look at the beauty of the beasts from the air.

He blew out another breath and started to formulate a plan.

"What are you doing?" Zach asked.

"I need to find a safe entry point to get on top of the glacier." What would it look like?

An hour and a half wasted away before they were on top of the glacier. The sight was awe-inspiring. He could imagine a glacier guide talking to the tourists. *This is one of several glaciers that flows from the Juneau Icefield.*

In the summer, Isaiah could have hoped to run across one of the tour groups. He wasn't sure if that would be a good thing or a bad thing. On the one hand, he might have been able to signal them to get help. On the other, anyone crossing their path would be in danger.

But it wasn't summer yet, and spring in this part of the world might as well be winter. He'd remained cognizant of the approaching storm clouds that would likely dump more snow on them. They were in a race against time now, and Isaiah wasn't hopeful they would win this.

He eyed the clouds once again and then gazed out over the river of ice ahead of them. He'd give it to Zach straight now and hopefully his brother, Jason, would make him listen.

"Crossing this glacier isn't going to be easy." As though navigating anything so monumental would be easy. "By far, it's the most treacherous thing we've faced. In the summer, maybe we could see all the dangers, but right now, there are plenty of crevasses and snow bridges hidden by layers of snow. That means we'll need to rope ourselves together, loop and hitch them for self-rescue, if required, and if that doesn't work, if one of us falls, the others can pull him or her out. But everything has to be tied right. We all have to be positioned a certain way, spaced apart as we cross, and there has to be tension in the ropes. Please listen very carefully as I give the instructions." It would take them some time just to get the ropes and harnesses and belay knots, for friction, tied just right.

This was going to be complicated. Isaiah squeezed the bridge of his nose. He couldn't get enough air, and he knew Heidi could relate.

"So what?" Jason asked. "We tie knots and rope ourselves together. Big deal."

Isaiah thought about what he'd read and learned about glaciers, and gave them the spiel, everything he knew and could remember, so they'd at least picture in their minds exactly what they were up against. Then he instructed them on roped movement across glacial terrain, fearing it was too much information at once.

He glanced at Heidi. "Did I forget anything?"

A nod accompanied her tenuous smile. "Our biggest danger is going to be crossing the snow bridges. It's when snow piles up over a crevasse so you can't see it. You could fall through. The glacier is filled with crevasses, so let's make sure we understand how to do this from the start. We cross crevasses we can see at right angles, unless they're small cracks, and then we just jump over them. And if we suspect a snow bridge is too weak to support us, then there's another technique we use."

Heidi sighed, and Isaiah knew she understood his concerns, as well. This was beyond technical for Jason and Zach.

"And then we cross carefully, one at a time."

Now did Zach see how long this would take them?

"Everyone needs an ice ax," Heidi added. "I think we have extras in the bags."

"Let's gear up then, and tread carefully, spread out and rope up." Isaiah got the rest of the gear out.

Though he wanted to tell Zach they weren't going to make it to the ice field in time, not before the storm rolled in, and not for his rendezvous, maybe it was best to let Zach see for himself. Isaiah didn't care to have Zach threaten Heidi's life yet again if he voiced his doubts.

When Isaiah started to tie Heidi on the rope, Zach yanked it away. "No. It's you, then me, then Heidi, then Jason. What's to keep you from dropping us into a crevasse and simply cutting the rope?"

Good point. Isaiah wished he'd thought of that himself.

The rope connecting her to Zach in front of her and Jason behind fully extended, Heidi put one foot in front of the other as they kept tension in the line.

Heidi was in top physical condition, and yet she wondered how much more of this she could take. Still, they were near the end of this nightmare. That both terrified her and kept her going. She had no idea what they would face once they actually made their destination and Zach's ride came to pick him up.

From where they were, as the glacier wound through the mountains like a big river of ice, she could see where it opened up into the Juneau Icefield. One of the largest in the world, it was the source of not only this glacier but forty larger glaciers that flowed outward, and scores of smaller ones, too. Funny to think the ice field encompassed hundreds of square miles and was rimmed by a temperate rainforest.

Where was Zach's rendezvous anyway? Crazy.

None of them had worried too much about where he planned to meet his buddy in the skiplane before, but if it was on the other side, he'd need to change the location. Especially with the threat of inclement weather. The sky began turning gray, clouds moving in over the sun as it started an early descent behind the mountains.

The wind whipped around Heidi. How she wished for a rescue today. She didn't want to spend yet another night with Zach, or another night in a tent surrounded by roaring wind and driving snow and arctic temperatures.

Zach yelled at Isaiah to move faster. He broke their line and moved ahead of Isaiah, tugging and yanking Heidi and Jason forward. Zach would get them all killed, including himself.

A sound broke through the wind. At the low whir of a single-engine plane, Heidi wanted to jump up and down. Wave her arms. But then she remembered.

Zach was expecting his ride. And they hadn't made the rendezvous, just as she knew they wouldn't.

In the distance, where blue sky met the clouds rushing in from the west, a ski-plane circled. Heidi couldn't know if it was the plane for Zach or just someone else.

But he was the one to jump up and down and wave and scream at the top of his lungs. The airplane circled back and flew away, growing smaller.

He cursed and kicked and shoved Isaiah into

the snow. Then he drew out his SAT phone and cursed some more. He couldn't get it to connect.

Isaiah stood and made his way to Heidi, stuck between Jason and Zach on the rope. "We need to find the safest place to make camp. We're too exposed out here, and the storm won't be forgiving."

"I know. But what about the ropes? Should we keep them on?"

He nodded. "For now."

"Zach!" Isaiah grabbed the man, gaining control over the situation.

Heidi's insides squeezed. She hoped Zach wouldn't react in a fit of rage and shoot Isaiah.

"He'll be back! You'll get your chance to call him. But right now, we have to set up the tents or we are going to die. You need to get your act together and focus on living through the night."

Jason nodded his agreement. "He's right, Zach. Let's prepare to weather another storm. If I never see the mountains or snow again it'll be too soon. But we're almost there. We almost made it. He can come back again for us later."

As far as Heidi could tell, this spot was as good as any for a camp. Isaiah assembled an avalanche probe he had with him to hopefully detect any hidden crevasse beneath them. Heidi, Isaiah and Jason worked to set up the tents. Jason tugged as much gear as he could into one.

The wind began to howl and the snow pricked her face like needles. Now they were down to two tents and four people. Would Zach notice the missing one?

God, please, I don't want to be stuck in a tent with Zach. He's crazy. She could only imagine in her worst nightmares what he might do to her.

Someone nudged her from behind. Heidi panicked and fought back. Then she realized it was Isaiah urging her inside the tent. She glanced over and spotted Jason watching. He gave a slight nod, as though he approved.

Zach was nowhere to be seen. Maybe he'd already climbed inside his own tent. With the storm and his need to make contact with his only ride out of here, he probably wouldn't think of Heidi until they were all buried in the storm.

When Heidi took too long to move inside the tent, Isaiah practically shoved her in.

"Stay there." He zipped the tent up.

God, please let Isaiah be the one who climbs into this tent. I don't want to weather this storm alone, but I don't want any of the others here. Isaiah was a good man. She'd always believed that, even after he'd hurt her. And she'd seen nothing but the best from him throughout this ordeal. He'd been strong enough to make the tough decisions, even when Heidi herself wasn't sure she could have done the same.

The wind whistled and the tent fluttered. Heidi's heart jumped around inside her, but she had enough experience that she shouldn't be so frightened. Her nerves were wearing thin; mostly because she didn't know what would happen next. She did know that she should only live one day at a time. One breath at a time, even. No one knew when their last moment in this world would be. In that way, everyone on the planet was terminal. Was it wrong to have so much left to do in this life? She didn't want to die. Not yet.

The zipper moved. Heidi held her breath. *Please, don't let it be Zach.*

Isaiah crawled in and Heidi's head swam, dizzy with relief.

"This is a blizzard all right. A whiteout. I'm going to have to crawl out every so often and dig us out. By the looks of it, maybe every fifteen minutes, half an hour. You know the drill. I reminded Jason about it. He's the only reasonable one over there."

"And…Zach?" Heidi couldn't voice the words, but she hoped Isaiah read her concern in her gaze.

"The storm will be too brutal for him to bother crawling out. That's why I convinced Jason to help keep the tents from getting buried." His gaze softened. "It's going to be a long, tough night. But trust me when I say, I will kill Zach with my bare hands before I let him lay a finger on you."

Guys had a way of talking bravado like that, but Heidi wanted to believe in Isaiah's fierce protective stance. She wanted to believe in him. Maybe he was the one guy who could save her, from more than just the likes of Zach. Maybe Isaiah could save her from her heartbroken world, even though he'd been part of it. But there had to be a reason he'd pushed her away. What was it?

He positioned himself on a sleeping bag, but didn't appear to get too comfortable. He must be exhausted, just like Heidi, but he couldn't afford to fall asleep. He'd need to dig them out. Heidi wouldn't let him shoulder that burden alone. She'd trade off with him.

But right now, only one thing burned in her mind and heart. "What happened to us, Isaiah?"

SEVENTEEN

The question knocked the breath from Isaiah.

Why did she think of that now, when they would battle for their lives tonight, and then tomorrow when they would come face-to-face with Zach, meeting either their destiny or demise?

His shoulders dropped as he deflated completely. How did he explain to her what had happened? He took off his gloves and raked his hands through his hair.

She stared at him, waiting.

"Now. You want to know all that now." It was a statement, not a question.

"I'm facing my mortality. I want to know if there could have been something more between us. And why there wasn't. Why did you pull away from me?"

Okay, so she was serious, and he understood her reasoning. He'd wanted a chance to tell her, to open up about his past so he could move on. But now he was chickening out.

"It's a long story."

"I've got all night."

He liked her spirit. But this night would drain him in more ways than one. He'd sort of hoped for an evening spent in her company just going over the trauma they'd been through. Working through it all. Making a plan for the big escape tomorrow. Then again, he had her full attention now. She couldn't run or walk away from what he had to say. She'd have to face him, and he'd be able to read her reaction.

"I know I'm asking a lot, being that we're in this tent and you're exhausted," she said. "And this is going to be awkward, but I'm a big girl. Right now, with everything that happened before and now this, I'm sinking fast and I need to climb out before it's too late. If I could just understand what happened, that would bring closure for me. Was it me? Or something completely unrelated?"

Intensity spilled from her big brown eyes. Soft eyes that were the windows to a soul full of love and compassion. No wonder Isaiah had struggled to let her go.

He wouldn't be holding anything back tonight. And Heidi would hate him when he was done.

"Okay, then. Here goes." Isaiah stared at his hands, wondering if he'd have to pull on the gloves and his coat and get outside before he could finish his story. "You need to know that all I've ever wanted to do was prove myself worthy of your family. I just wanted to move on and leave my past behind. I didn't want to make another mistake, especially with you."

He glanced up from his hands to read Heidi's face. Slightly flushed. She'd understood him, then. She'd been right to suspect that this was all about his feelings for her.

"It's okay. I'm not going to judge you. Just tell me." Her voice was gentle, pleading.

Isaiah wished for another time and place in which to tell her. He prayed for the chance to have more with her, maybe even the rest of his life. The thought made his breath hitch. He couldn't wish for more.

"I have to dig us out first, then I'll tell you the rest."

"What? You're kidding, right?"

"No, I'm not. You hear that?" He pressed his hand against the side of the tent. "It's heavy with snow. But don't worry, I'll be right back."

He put on his gloves and the rest of his winter gear and scrambled from the tent into the blasting whiteout, darkness quickly falling. He had barely enough battery power in his headlamp to assist him, but at least he still had the night vision goggles. He'd loaned a pair to Jason, too.

But more than needing to scrape away the snow piling over the tent almost faster than he could dig, he needed time to think through his response to Heidi. He knew he'd have to explain one day, but he hadn't expected her question tonight.

Brutally cold wind blasted him, making it hard to stand against the force. Driving snow quickly buried both tents. Where was Jason? Isaiah risked a hike over and yelled against the tent, "Get out here and dig yourself out if you want to live!"

In all his time living in Montana and in Alaska, he'd never weathered anything like this.

He hiked back to the tent where Heidi was cocooned inside. *God, help me keep her alive, help protect her from the forces of nature, and from the evil in the tent next door. I don't know what tomorrow will bring, and tonight has enough troubles of its own, as You say in Your Word. And Lord, please help me give the right answer when I speak the truth. Let it not just be more hurt for Heidi.*

The anguish in his heart and his prayer made the time he spent digging pass fast. Too fast, actually. Now he had to head back inside and spill his story, the full of it.

As quietly as he could, he slipped back into the tent, snow blowing past him. Heidi's eyes

blinked open. Had she been asleep? He regretted waking her. She needed the rest and besides that, he didn't relish telling her what she
wanted to know.

Heidi sat up, looking disheveled.

"Why don't you get some rest?" He settled
on the sleeping bag at the far side of the tent.
He couldn't afford to close his eyes or he might
never wake up.

"It's my turn, you know. I'm going out next."

Isaiah shook his head. He couldn't be certain
that only Jason would dig his tent out. "I don't
want you to run into Zach out there. I don't want
him to have a reason to think about you."

"You can't do this on your own all night. I'll
wear your coat, make him think it's you. How
about that?"

He scratched his jaw. "That might work."

She smiled. "Don't think you're getting out
of telling me the story. So give."

He sighed. Might as well dive in. "Before I
moved to Mountain Cove, I fell in love with
someone, only I found out later that she was
engaged."

Isaiah heard Heidi's quick intake of breath. He
wouldn't avoid her gaze now. He would watch
her with every word he said. The story would
sound much too similar to her own betrayal,

and he could hardly bear it. But let the blame fall where it may.

"When I found out, I confronted her, of course. She said she wasn't sure she wanted to get married after all and, well, a guy could hope. I guess I thought maybe she loved me and would break things off with her fiancé. Still, she saw me in secret. He knew nothing about us, and for that..." Isaiah hung his head. Shame filled him. "It was wrong. I know that now. Because then Aaron found out about us."

Heidi kept perfectly still, but her eyes grew wide.

"I thought it was over between them, and I would have a chance with her. I should have backed out of the situation completely from the beginning. I kept telling myself they weren't married so it wasn't cheating. She didn't leave him, and she didn't break things off with me, either."

"What happened?" Heidi's soft voice broke through the images Isaiah had fought hard to leave behind.

He wasn't sure he could answer. He needed to dig them out again. Find the words. "I found her body."

Heidi gasped, pressed her palms against her mouth.

Isaiah stood and left the tent before she could

gather her thoughts. She was supposed to go out next and scrape the snow drifts away.

"Oh, Isaiah," she whispered. And that poor girl. What could have happened to her? She couldn't imagine how awful that must have been for her family, and for Isaiah to find her like that. And to have been part of a betrayal...

Memories of her own experience with Lon surfaced. He'd made her feel as if he cared about her, during one of the lowest times of her life, and assured her they were going somewhere in their relationship. Of course, she knew now she'd only been on the rebound from Isaiah. She hadn't even kissed Isaiah yet, but there was just something so powerful between them that it far outweighed her relationship with Lon. But she'd tried to run from the pain. And then the day Isaiah had told her that Lon was married had nearly been the worst day of her life.

It didn't help matters that the Warren siblings had learned the devastating news of their father's infidelity in recent months. Heidi's anger burned against Lon, as it had against her father, though it was through her father's death that Cade had uncovered the news that he had cheated on their mother, and that they could have a half brother or half sister out there somewhere.

How could Heidi have been so stupid? Why couldn't someone have told her before she'd gotten involved?

Still, Lon wasn't from Mountain Cove and didn't live there. He'd been camping at his cabin on an island along the channel, and she'd met him when he'd aided the SAR team on an island rescue.

She could hear Isaiah scraping the snow off outside, and the tent shuddered, pulling her thoughts back.

To find out he'd been part of a similar betrayal—no wonder he kept that to himself. No wonder he didn't feel he could ever share that with Heidi. Still, he'd pulled away long before Lon had stepped into her life so there had to be more.

He unzipped the flap and stepped in, bringing the cold and snow in along with his drawn features. Isaiah didn't even look up at her, just went to his place on the sleeping bag. And said nothing.

"I need to know the rest, if you don't mind."

"What do you think happened? I was devastated, of course. I loved her." He pressed his hand over his eyes.

An ice ax dug into Heidi's heart.

"But she'd hurt me, by stringing me along.

I'd been an idiot. So I went to her to tell her we were over. I was afraid for her life, too. I learned she had doubts about her engagement because her fiancé was a violent man. I didn't want him to hurt her because of me. And in the end, that's exactly what happened. But did they arrest him? No. I was the one who became a person of interest. Almost a suspect then."

"And now?" *Oh, Lord, please don't let it be that he is in hiding. That he ran away.* She couldn't bear to hear that.

She studied him. He wasn't a murderer. No. Never. She wouldn't believe that.

"The police were never able to find enough evidence to pin things on me or her fiancé, though I know he must have murdered her." Finally he looked at her. "But you see, it doesn't matter that I'm innocent. I live in the shadow of those events. I feel like I helped her betray her future husband, and because of that, she's dead. Because of me. I didn't pull the trigger on the gun, but what's the difference? I played a part in her death. Maybe I could have prevented it. Could have been there when he shot and killed her. Taken the bullet for her instead."

"You don't mean that, Isaiah." As horrified as Heidi felt from hearing that story, her heart went out to him.

"Yes…" He nodded. Searched her eyes. "Yes,

I do. And even though I didn't kill her, as far as the town was concerned, I might as well have. They were suspicious of me. The gossips couldn't just drop the story. The newspapers and media wouldn't leave me alone. I had to change my name and start over. I thought that I could leave it all behind and make a new life."

Heidi hated the tears brimming in her eyes. But she wouldn't swipe them away. She wouldn't look away from Isaiah. But she said nothing. There were no words to comfort him. There were no words to express the battle that raged in her soul.

"Now you see why I never told you. I thought I had to keep it all hidden away to move on. Then as we got closer, I knew that I couldn't keep that from you. After what I'd been through I didn't want to make another mistake when it came to love. I wanted everything to be out in the open. But how could I tell you? I knew you would be hurt. And you deserve much better than me. I had to pull away from you to…"

"To protect me." Because he cared. He'd even said the word *love*. Had Isaiah loved her? Did he still, even now?

"And then you were so devastated when you learned about your father's infidelity, and after what happened between you and Lon, well, that only confirmed to me that I had done the right thing. After hearing all that, what do you think about us now?" Isaiah huffed, clearly disillusioned.

As she was. "I think it's my turn to dig."

Without looking at Isaiah, Heidi pulled on her gloves, hat, coat and boots and crawled from the tent. The hurt she'd inflicted on Isaiah by giving him such a lame response backfired and zinged through her. She was more than heartbroken over his story. She was hurt for him. Hurt for herself.

She'd held on to the slightest hope that he could make her believe in everlasting love again. But no. He'd only confirmed that love would eventually fail her, if she ever chose to risk her heart again.

"Why, God?" she shouted into the storm. She'd wanted an answer from Isaiah, but she hadn't in her wildest dreams been prepared for this.

As if leaving Cade to survive on his own in this storm wasn't enough. Watching Zach leave his girlfriend behind wasn't enough. As if being abducted like this wasn't enough.

Emotionally obliterated, Heidi wanted to lie down and let the snow bury her. It would only take a few minutes, tops.

Despite the frigid temperatures, she worked up a sweat beneath her thermal coat while digging the snow away with the pack shovel. Of course, she'd forgotten to switch coats with Isaiah, but she could care less about Zach seeing her anymore.

Her muscles burned. Lungs screamed. How had she even for one second allowed herself to think that Isaiah could be the man to pull her out of the abyss, to help her trust in love again? He was the absolute last person she should ever care about. He'd participated in the very thing she loathed, been party to cheating on a loved one. Sure, the woman had only been engaged, but it had all been a lie. Heidi couldn't begin to imagine the pain her fiancé had felt.

Had that driven the man to kill his intended?

She thought about her own father cheating on her mother. And she could have another sibling out there somewhere. The tears were freezing on her cheeks. Heidi had to stop freaking out.

She threw her arms up and looked into the raging storm. "Why, God?" she cried again.

Once she scraped snow from the other side of the tent, she would be done, at least for a few more minutes. But she wasn't sure what purpose that would serve. The cold reality of their situation churned inside her once again, and this time, she couldn't shake it off. They were going to die. She could feel it in her bones. If not by Zach's hand, then because of this storm.

They'd come this far, yes, but Heidi's strength had drained away to almost nothing, then Isaiah's story had taken the rest. She was broken and freezing. Her limbs grew numb with cold. She could barely dig anymore, her efforts having no effect. Growing more sluggish by the second, she fought hard to care.

She was frozen with pain and could not bring herself to cry out for help, or even pray anymore. Yes, she knew God had been there with them, leading them, guiding them. But how much more could she take? It was one thing to battle the elements and Zach, but it was quite another to also fight the emotional and spiritual onslaught that threatened to topple her.

Heidi tumbled into the deep white stuff.

For a moment, she sat there, letting the driving snow pelt her, pile on top of her.

Bury her.

"God, I can't do this. I can't deal with this anymore. What do you want from me?"

Suddenly, a sense of calm came quietly into her spirit, even as the storm raged around her.

That was just like Him, she knew.

Eyes closed, lashes sticking to her moist but soon-to-be frozen cheeks, she nodded. "Okay, Jesus, I'm all Yours. I can't do this alone."

She couldn't lie to herself again, either. Despite her best efforts to protect her heart, she loved Isaiah. Even after everything he'd told her and knowing he wasn't the right man for her. She couldn't count on someone like him for a love that would last forever, but still, she loved him.

Isn't that kind of like You, God? You love us even though we fail You time and again. I want to love like that, God, You hear me? I don't want to care about Isaiah's past.

But she did. God help her, she did care that he'd been involved in a betrayal with someone. That the police thought he might have murdered her. And she wouldn't let herself love him. But none of that mattered as Heidi grew sleepy and the snow blanketed her. Somewhere inside her tormented psyche, she knew she had to get up or she would die.

But she couldn't move.

EIGHTEEN

He hadn't wanted to let her dig. Too many dangers out there. But he couldn't stop her, either. Truth was he'd fall over with exhaustion if he didn't have some help. But this hadn't been the way he'd wanted it.

He felt the furrow between his brows all the way to his toes and back up to his heart.

These past three, nearly four, years that he'd lived in Mountain Cove, he'd never looked back to his hometown in Montana. Well, except to phone his folks once in a while. Fortunately, his parents had bought a ranch and retired on the other side of the state before any of the "happenings," as they referred to it. Though they'd never made him feel unwelcome, he couldn't let go of the fact that he'd brought shame to them. All the more reason to change his name. But he was their only child and having him take another name had to hurt, as well.

He hadn't been back to see them until this

past Christmas. Being with his family, and away from Heidi and hers, had given him some perspective. Time to come to grips with the fact that she deserved better than a guy who'd made the ugly mistake he'd made. A mistake that had cost a life. Ultimately, the police hadn't blamed him, but he blamed himself. If he'd never met her, never become involved with her, she'd still be alive.

And then Isaiah had to go through the pain of closing himself off emotionally from Heidi—he'd never known that kind of pain, watching her hurt, and being the cause of it. She never said much, but he'd seen the torment pouring from her eyes as hard as the driven snow. But it was for the best. For her, he'd kept telling himself. The knife only twisted deeper when she took up with a new guy. The entire Warren family was wary of the relationship, but Heidi had already been through so much that no one dared to say anything. That is, until Isaiah overheard the man on his cell phone talking to his wife one day. Isaiah had been the one to tell Heidi.

Nothing could ever be worse than finding the body of someone you cared about. Nothing. But hurting Heidi had come close. Watching her go through it all had only confirmed to him that he should keep his distance, and he should keep his secrets.

He glanced at his watch. She was due back about now, and he needed to be prepared for whatever she would dish out.

Raking his hands through the hair at his temple, he squeezed, pressing in hard. He wasn't sure how things had come full circle, and he'd somehow been persuaded to tell her everything.

But he did know that her reaction hadn't been a surprise. He'd deluded himself into allowing an ounce of hope that maybe things could work between them. Maybe this fierce love that burned inside wasn't for nothing. People lied to themselves and would use any excuse to justify something they really wanted. Isaiah was no different.

He sat up. Heidi was taking much too long. Zach…

She'd forgotten to switch into Isaiah's coat.

He donned his gloves and coat again and scrambled from the tent. Wearing his night vision goggles, he stomped around outside, panic engulfing him. Where was she? It had been much too long. Snow was already packing up high around the tent. A glance over at the other one told him someone had continued to dig the snow away.

"Heidi, where are you?" he called.

Oh, Lord, please help me find her!

He started toward the far side of the shelter and stumbled over something.

Oh, no…

Isaiah dropped to his knees. "Heidi!"

God in heaven, please don't let her die.

Isaiah scraped snow from her, his pulse slamming his temples. He lifted her seemingly lifeless frozen form into his arms and carried her back into the tent. He'd waited too long to check on her. What an idiot he'd been. He shouldn't have let her outside to dig, but after what he'd told her, she needed time alone to process the news, and he'd let her have her way.

He checked her pulse. Still alive. He laid her on the sleeping bag, her blue lips terrifying him. "Heidi, wake up!"

He wasn't exactly sure what had happened. She was dressed well enough, but hypothermia could still be a risk in this weather. Maybe she had simply succumbed to exhaustion. He checked her vitals again, and searched for any obvious injury. No bump on the head. Her pulse was good and steady. Her skin didn't feel cold and more color returned to her lips. *Come on, come on, come on, Heidi. Wake up.* Other than keeping her warm there wasn't anything else he could do, except pray, and he'd never stopped doing that.

Isaiah knew he needed to dig some more,

keep them from being buried alive, but he didn't want to leave Heidi. He zipped her into the sleeping bag, warm and snug. There was nothing more he could do for her.

Isaiah glanced back one more time before unzipping the tent to crawl out.

Her eyelids fluttered and she gazed at him. His heart leaped with relief.

Since finding her passed out in the snow, he'd completely forgotten about what he'd shared with her moments before. The pain in her eyes as she looked at him now brought it rolling back and into him, the force nearly knocking him over. He had to harden his heart.

He turned his attention back to exiting the tent.

"Isaiah," she whispered.

He froze, unsure that he wanted to face her. "Yeah."

"We need to leave tonight. Now. Zach is going to kill us tomorrow."

Had she forgotten about Isaiah's confession? Didn't she realize she would have died out there if he hadn't found her in time? She wasn't thinking clearly. The temperatures and the storm were more brutal than anything else they'd endured through this entire ordeal. She would die if they left this tent and hiked in the storm tonight. They both would.

"Better to bide our time and face off with Zach tomorrow. We wouldn't survive this weather." Isaiah left her to think on his words.

Heidi opened her eyes, unsure of what woke her. Tucked deep in the warm sleeping bag, she'd long ago shed her coat, but she couldn't remember where she was.

Then it all rushed back.

Only the wind wasn't howling. The storm had blown through.

The zipper again. Someone was coming inside the tent. The terror of Zach's unwanted attention rushed back at her, too. She pushed out of the sleeping bag and got into the most defensive position she could, given the small space.

Isaiah crawled inside. "Good, you're awake. We're packing up. Have to make it onto the ice field today, to Zach's coordinates. Just a little longer, Heidi."

She shrugged into her coat and grabbed her boots, her head spinning as memories of last night—everything Isaiah had told her—flooded back.

"Are you okay?"

She flicked her gaze at him, then back to her boots. "Sure. I must have slept like a rock. What did I miss?"

This time, she let her gaze linger. Something in his reaction held a question.

"No, really. Did I miss something?"

"No." He grinned.

Heidi shook off the effect it had on her. She needed time to think through all he'd told her. She'd wanted an answer. Wanted to know why he'd thrown away their friendship. Well, now she knew, and she fully understood why he'd distanced himself instead of telling her the truth. She would have done the same thing. Maybe.

She rolled up her bag. "Give me a sec."

"Heidi." He cleared his throat.

She didn't want to look at him, but realization dawned and she risked a glance up, seeing the haggard expression he'd tried to hide with his grin. "I must have slept through the whole night. Isaiah, I'm so sorry. You must be exhausted."

He nodded, a slight tuck of his chin. "A few more hours and this will be over. Knowing that will keep me going. But I'm more worried about you."

"Don't be."

"Heidi, don't you remember? You went out to dig and you never came back. I found you passed out, half-buried in the snow. Do you remember anything?"

Heidi finished with the sleeping bag and let

her mind drift back to those last few moments of digging. She'd been praying, crying out to God, then finally given her burdens to Him. But she'd stopped moving, and maybe all the sweat she'd worked up from digging had dropped her body temperature even lower. It was all hazy now, but she'd been tired. So very tired.

"What's going on in there?" Zach banged on the tent. "Let's get moving."

Heidi shared a look with Isaiah and in his eyes she saw he hoped as much as she did that they would live to finish this conversation.

They crawled out and packed the bags.

"We can leave all this," Zach said. "Get a move on. I can't afford to miss my plane this time. There's a short window before another storm. Talked to my contact last night. Curse this blasted region of the world."

Isaiah glanced up at the sky and Heidi followed his gaze. Did an odd mixture of expectation and dread roil in his gut, too? She could feel this ordeal winding down to its gritty ending. Searchers were out there, combing the mountains. David and Adam wouldn't stop searching until they found their siblings, but even they couldn't search in a storm.

And even if they looked over the ice field, they were talking fifteen hundred square miles. But surely they would be able to narrow that down to a few hundred, as if that would make a difference.

"Heidi and I'll have the basics packed up in a few. We can't afford to leave this in case things go wrong. It's a matter of survival."

Zach railed at them and Jason stepped into the fray. "They're right. Just in case he doesn't show up, we could die without the tents and supplies."

Thank goodness Jason was able to reason with his disagreeable brother. After they packed the gear, they roped themselves up and spaced apart, just like yesterday, in order to be safe as they crossed snow bridges.

They hiked through a maze of visible crevasses, and sometimes had to backtrack, but in spring, despite the storms that insisted on blasting through, a lot of the snow had melted on parts of the glacier. And yet dangers remained hidden beneath the snow. She had to pay attention, stay alert, but her energy had been drained long ago. Like Isaiah, she told herself she could make it to the end, which would come up on them much too fast.

In the distance, she could see where the glacier spilled from the ice field, which was really just a huge valley of interconnected glaciers, and the higher mountain peaks broke through. She saw the summit of Devil's Paw and Michael's Sword, gleaming snow-free in the distance, much closer now than she'd seen from miles away several nights ago. The nunataks, or rocky parts of the peaks, faced off as if in an eternal battle.

Heidi felt as though she were in an eternal battle herself.

God, I don't know what's ahead of us, but I ask for Your help and guidance over the next few hours. And I ask for Your help again, in knowing what to think about Isaiah's story. Help him to forgive himself, and help me to let it go. I'm not sure any of it even matters, considering we might both be dead in the next few hours.

A scripture drifted across her heart.

"...Because he has anointed me to proclaim good news to the poor. He has sent me to proclaim freedom for the prisoners and recovery of sight for the blind, to set the oppressed free..."

Lord, if ever captives needed setting free, that would be me and Isaiah.

Her thoughts went immediately to Cade and Rhea, though the two of them had never been far from her mind and heart.

Zach tugged on the rope, jerking Heidi forward and out of her thoughts. She'd been hiking too slowly for him.

In the distance, the sound of a small prop plane drew all gazes up. Heidi's pulse ramped up. Was it searchers?

Or Zach's personal rescuer?

Heidi got her answer. The plane circled lower and around them. She spotted Zach giving a thumbs-up. "Okay, people, let's get this train moving."

Again he tugged on the rope and Isaiah picked up the pace ahead of them, as well.

Her heart tripped over itself with dread. Zach only needed them to assist him over the dangerous parts of the glacier and then once on the ice field, when he had his plane waiting, he would shoot them both.

How could it end any other way?

Heidi was nearly breathless when they finally spotted the ski-plane landing in the distance. The guy obviously knew what he was doing. She was curious to know who the pilot was, but then again, that was just one more reason she and Isaiah had to die today, as far as Zach was concerned.

In front of her, Zach stopped, turned and made his way back to Heidi.

Oh, no. Here it comes. He's going to kill me now. Oh, God, what do I do? Help me!

When Isaiah's rope grew taut, he turned around.

Zach grabbed Heidi and pulled her close. Isaiah kept hiking toward them, rage burning behind his eyes. Heidi tried to free herself from Zach but he only tightened his grip.

And Isaiah kept hiking. He was almost on them.

Zach took a few steps back.

"This is where we part ways," he said. "And I'm taking Heidi with me."

"What?" Heidi's pulse jumped. She tried to tear away from him.

He pulled her closer and reached for the gun in his pocket.

NINETEEN

Isaiah lunged at Zach.

No more waiting until the right moment. This was do-or-die.

Zach tugged his weapon out, fired off a shot and missed.

Isaiah was on him, fighting for control of the firearm. He'd warned Zach to spare his ammunition in order to save Cade and Rhea's lives, but now Isaiah and Heidi had to face the bullets. He knocked the weapon away and it slid across the ice. Heidi ran for it but she was tied to Zach and the ropes were tangled.

Jason had a gun, too, but couldn't shoot at Isaiah with Zach on him. Isaiah didn't think Jason was a killer anyway. He pulled Isaiah away from Zach, and while he struggled to reach his weapon buried inside the coat beneath the layers of the rope and harness, Isaiah and Zach ran for the gun on the ice.

Isaiah pulled Zach back with the rope. He

couldn't let him reach it first. Zach turned his attention back to Isaiah and plowed into him. They went down hard against the snow-packed ice. Pain coursed through Isaiah's face and head, magnified by the deep freeze beneath him. Jason appeared in his vision.

He couldn't fight two of them off. But he couldn't let Zach take Heidi with him, either. He'd die fighting.

She tried to pull Jason away from him, but Jason threw her back. It was a tangled mess since they were all tied together. Why hadn't Zach just taken his money and gone to the plane? Heidi's scream ripped through the air, and maybe even the ice under him. He could swear he felt it vibrate beneath him, accompanied by a deep rumble.

Oh, no!

Zach slammed his fist into Isaiah's face and the blood poured from his nose. Zach's face was bruised and bloodied, too. At least Isaiah had given as good as he'd gotten. To Jason, too. But then he noticed Heidi's swollen lip. Isaiah tried to shove Zach away.

And then it was over.

Zach stood up, staggered a little and backed away. The iced shuddered and shifted. Was the glacier moving? Zach, Jason and Heidi struggled to remain standing. Isaiah saw now what a losing battle this had been from the beginning. Two guys against one.

Then the ground beneath Isaiah caved in.

The snow and ice gave way, revealing a hidden crevasse. That was the whole reason for the ropes. They weren't in the correct formation and they would all go down if Zach didn't react.

"Use your axes!" Heidi yelled.

Isaiah couldn't get to his ice ax and, though he grappled with his gloves against the edge, he couldn't gain traction and finally fell back, free-falling, pulling them all down with him.

Screams erupted from above as the ropes slid across the ice.

A yawning, dark abyss rose up toward the bluer ice of the crevasse as if to close its jaws around him, filling him with terror. But the rope grew taught, jerking Isaiah. Someone had been quick thinking enough to stop the spiral into the crevasse.

Above him, Zach clung to the edge. He'd managed to get his ice ax in time, and crawled out. Or maybe Heidi had been able to toss it to him. Regardless, he would make it out.

Isaiah worked to free himself from the pack on his back that would weigh him down. In his worst nightmares, he had never imagined he would be the one in the crevasse, waiting to be rescued by this group. They could pull him out. But he didn't plan to wait on them.

Either way, getting out would take Isaiah time he didn't have. He dangled in the crevasse by a rope connected to two men who wanted him dead. He dropped the one remaining pack off his back, decreasing his personal weight so he could climb out, but it dangled from the rope, attached by a carabiner. The other pack he'd been carrying, but had dropped in his scuffle with Zach and Jason, had already fallen into the chasm.

He eyed the blue ice beneath him. Beautiful. God's splendor could be seen even here in the unlikeliest of places. He took it all in, wishing he could have been exposed to this amazing sight under much different circumstances. Terror grappled with a strange peace inside him. This could be it for him. This could be his death. The way his life ended. Not a bullet like he'd expected. But by a fall into these icy depths.

A few verses from Psalm 139 floated out of his heart and into his thoughts. *"Where can I go from your Spirit? Where can I flee from your presence? If I go up to the heavens, you are there; if I make my bed in the depths, you are there."*

If Isaiah fell, God would be there.

The rope budged, pulling him toward the

edge. What? He couldn't believe it. They were actually going to save him? Had to be Heidi with her persuasive power over Zach. *God, please don't let her sacrifice herself for me.*

He made it to a ledge of hanging ice. Heidi carefully inched toward him and handed him an ice ax. "Use this, while we pull you out."

Isaiah took the tool and speared the ice with it.

Didn't she realize that Zach wasn't going to let him live? And Isaiah had used up his last chance to save them. Maybe this was the way it was supposed to end, and justice was being served. Isaiah was getting what he'd had coming to him all along for the part he'd played in Leslie's death.

"You have to survive this, Heidi. Do whatever it takes. Do you hear me?"

Heidi's tears dropped onto the snow. "No, you're not going to die. I won't let you. I can't lose you, too!"

Isaiah couldn't stand to hear her sobs, and he would keep fighting, keep trying, just for her. But he couldn't see a way out of this. Still, he latched onto the ice with the ax to haul himself up, knowing that in the end, it wouldn't matter. He should say what he had to say before it was too late.

"I'm sorry that I couldn't get us out of this. I love you. I think I always have."

There. He'd told her before it was too late. Well, sort of. Isaiah had probably waited too long to tell Heidi, and all the reasons for holding back seemed ridiculous now. He was within seconds of his life ending.

"Let's go, sweetheart."

Heidi tried to untie the rope attaching her to the madman as he dragged her away from the edge. He and Jason had prevented Isaiah from tumbling farther into the crevasse to begin with, since they were all tied together.

Why was the guy waiting to kill him?

Heidi watched in horror as Zach edged toward Isaiah with the gun.

She wouldn't let Zach kill Isaiah. She'd sooner die with him, for him.

Zach had a thing for her? Well, she would do as Isaiah suggested. Survive no matter what it took. Save Isaiah, no matter what it took.

"Zach, please, no. Don't shoot him. I'll go with you. I *want* to go with you. I won't cause you any trouble." Heidi softened her voice, going for an alluring tone.

That got his attention, his gaze drifting over to her. At the look in his eyes, nausea swirled in her stomach. She wasn't sure what she was doing, making a deal with evil. "But you can't shoot Isaiah."

A lump swelled in her throat. She didn't want to go with Zach willingly, but she didn't know what else to do.

"You have a deal, sweetheart." Zach tugged out a knife, the blade flashing when the sun peeked through the clouds.

"What…what are you doing?" She couldn't believe he would twist her words around like some sick joke, but she should have known better.

What a fool Heidi had been. Zach didn't have to shoot Isaiah. *Oh, Isaiah, please use that ice ax I gave you. Hold on a little longer.*

Zach pressed the blade against the climbing ropes.

Isaiah's eyes flicked to Heidi. He held her gaze—his own conveying the love he'd held back from her all this time. Heidi wanted—no, needed—more time with him. This couldn't be happening.

"See? I'm a man of my word. I'm not going to shoot him."

She screamed, "No!"

Zach cut the rope.

Isaiah held on with the ax, but Zach shoved him into the crevasse.

Isaiah flailed back into the blue ice until it

turned black and she could no longer see him. Dumbfounded, she looked on, shock squeezing the life from her body. When Zach pulled her away, she fought and kicked.

"What did you do that for, Zach?" Jason asked. "Why didn't you just shoot him?"

"No one could survive that fall. He's as good as dead, idiot. If he survives, which I doubt, he can't get out. They'll never find him in there. Besides, that was more elegant than shooting him."

Panic and tears engulfed Heidi. Her knees buckled beneath her. Jason and Zach held her up, dragging her toward the plane in the distance. She didn't want their help.

The Bible said that vengeance was the Lord's, but her grief and sorrow would kill her. Better to let the anger, her need for revenge carry her forward. She would get even with Zach, if it was the last thing she did. He would pay for killing Isaiah. Leaving Cade behind with Rhea. For kidnapping her, and worse—for the lives of the two men she loved the most in the world.

Her brother Cade, with whom she'd always been the closest. And Isaiah.

Isaiah...

She already knew she could never overpower these men or get the upper hand as long as they held the weapons. Isaiah had already tried twice and failed. And yet he was still a hero to her. She wouldn't let Isaiah's or Cade's sacrifices be in vain.

The wind picked up again, and a few flecks of snow hit her cheeks. In the distance, she heard the prop plane starting up. Zach and Jason picked up their pace.

"Unless you want me to leave you behind, too, you need to walk on your own." He released Heidi.

She wanted to rail at him, but that wouldn't work with her plan.

"Okay, let's go." Heidi took off, leaving the two men behind. She was in better shape than either of them and had only lost her strength momentarily due to the gravity of her loss.

Heidi knew better than the two men that their window of opportunity to get rescued was quickly closing. Finally, they made it to the plane and dropped the gear they'd carried with them. The pilot climbed out and shook hands with Zach and Jason.

"You got the money?"

Zach nodded, pointing to the green vinyl bag he'd never let out of his sight.

The guy grinned. "Get it loaded."

"You heard him." Zach eyed Heidi. She was his slave now. "Load the packs."

"All of it? Some of it belongs to the SAR team." As if that mattered anymore.

Zach obviously wanted to rid himself of every shred of evidence of his involvement with the missing SAR team and would dump the packs as far from here as possible. Heidi wasn't sure the small plane could carry all their heavy packs *and* the passengers.

Fine with her.

She hefted the bags and carried them over to the open door under the wing. That's when she spotted the money bag and knew what to do.

There was only one way to truly hurt Zach.

Heidi removed the green bag and hid it under the other bags. She piled the rest of them into the plane, while kicking snow and ice over the green pack.

"Are you almost done? We have to go." Jason climbed into the front seat, as did the pilot.

Zach squeezed her shoulder and slipped by her. He offered his hand. "Come on, sweetheart. Get in and close the door. We're going to beat the storm this time." He grinned as if he thought he could charm her.

Heidi lifted the last bag and stuffed it inside. She climbed in next to Zach. This was the moment she had to play things just right. All would be lost or won on this move.

Moisture surged from her palms. Her pulse

raced. Would Zach notice her increased breathing? Panic threatened to take over as she gasped for breath.

No, not now. She had to make this work.

Still, maybe he would think her reaction normal, considering that she'd climbed into an airplane with a murderer and his friends.

Heidi pushed down her anxiety, gained control over her breathing and smiled back. In the seat, she inched forward slowly, drawing Zach's full attention. Letting him believe she would kiss him.

Why would he for one second fall for that? Guys could be so stupid. When she was mere inches from Zach's lips, she fought to control her gag reflex. Heidi slid her hand into his coat pocket where he'd left his weapon loosely hanging for easy access, just like she'd watched him do a hundred times on their journey. She also knew he always had a round chambered. Without that, her plan wouldn't work. Though she tugged on his jacket a little, he never noticed, too focused on her lips and proximity.

Heidi pointed the gun at Zach's temple before he realized what was going on.

"Okay, this is what's going to happen now. I'm getting off this plane and you men are flying away into the sunset without me."

Zach acted as though he might move to take

the gun from her, but Heidi chose this moment to show her true strength. She pressed the muzzle hard and fast against his temple until he cowered.

"Yeah, sure, lady, whatever you want," the pilot said.

"We don't need her, Zach," Jason agreed. "But it's your head."

He snickered at his joke and would probably pay for that later.

"We have the money, man, just let her go."

Zach scowled, the look in his eyes foreboding. He wasn't done with her yet. Wasn't ready to let her go. In his gaze, she could read well enough that he'd had plans for her. Heidi slid away from him, but was unable to tear her eyes from the evil look in his. She used his tunnel vision to her advantage as she lifted the last pack she'd loaded and tossed it to the ground. "I'm taking this pack for myself. I need to survive the storm."

Zach didn't want anyone to live to tell their story. But he was out of options now.

She dropped the pack on top of the already buried mound. Closing the airplane door, she backed away, continuing to point the weapon at Zach's head through the window of the skiplane. Likely his pilot had another weapon inside, but maybe not. She wasn't sure what had happened to the other weapons Jason and Zach carried, but no one moved to shoot her. Regardless, they didn't have time to waste on Heidi as the wind picked up. If the pilot waited even a minute longer, they wouldn't leave the ice field.

They couldn't afford to battle it out with her.

Nor could she afford for them to stay.

The plane moved forward and away. As she memorized the registration number along the fuselage, she kicked more snow over the green bag, but it was also hidden under the pack she'd kept for herself. If Zach thought to look for his money in the next few moments, she was in big trouble.

But he didn't.

The plane droned off into the distance until she no longer heard it. She released a breath and tried to slow her heart, but she had lost so much. How did she wrap her heart and mind around it?

And she was all alone. She had only thought she was alone in the dark place she'd lingered over the past months. That was nothing compared to this. Heidi had never imagined herself alone in the middle of the barren, snow-covered ice field.

Her thoughts jumbled together as her predicament overwhelmed her. But Heidi sucked her breaths in slowly and focused on living. She had to survive this to tell Cade's story in case he couldn't. She had to survive to tell Isaiah's story.

Her heart cried over her loss, but she opened up the pack.

Oh, no...this bag didn't hold a tent. She'd miscalculated.

Looking up at the sky she watched the clouds quickly gathering. An unwelcome sight. If she wasn't rescued soon, she would die from exposure.

Oh, God, I've been an idiot!

All she could think about was getting back at Zach by taking the money away from him. Taking the one thing he loved away. And now here she was, stuck on the ice field with no way to live. She couldn't decide if this was better than being on that plane with Zach.

She doubted burning the money would buy her much time. She'd have to build an ice cave, but for that, she'd need an ax—the one she'd given to Isaiah.

Isaiah.

Carrying the pack with climbing gear and the bag of money, Heidi hiked toward the approaching storm clouds, snow mixed with some rain chilling her to the core.

God, if you have any plans for me to be rescued or to survive this, it had better be soon.

Finally, Heidi found the crevasse where Isaiah

had met his demise. A small flame of hope ignited in her heart. Maybe he was still alive in there. She could climb down to him and haul him back up.

"Isaiah!" she called. Her voice bounced off the brilliant blue walls. Cerulean walls that lied to her, claiming their purity and innocence. But with several more calls out to Isaiah and no echoing reply, her hopes died until she knew the truth. This crevasse was a killer.

TWENTY

Isaiah woke up to dim lighting in the distance.

He blinked, taking in his surroundings, trying to remember where he was.

He must have fallen in his attempt to climb from the crevasse. When Zach had shoved him the rest of the way in, Isaiah thought he would plummet to his death, but he'd landed against a channel where water poured, like an ice luge, and simply slid the rest of the way deeper into the crevasse. That had saved his life.

Only problem was, the fall had broken his leg.

Despite the last words Isaiah had given Heidi, he wasn't about to stay here and give up. So he found a way to crawl and dealt with his injury. Pulling the ropes and gear he needed to attempt to scale the ice-walled crevasse, Isaiah began to work his way up when the ice gave and he plummeted.

The pain in his leg gut-wrenching and angry, Isaiah used focused breathing to push away the darkness edging his vision like death closing in. He had more fight left in him than he thought possible, but maybe that had something to do with the light at the bottom of the crevasse.

It was odd, really, to look down and expect darkness but to see light instead.

That gave him hope.

There was another way out. But he'd have to go deeper. There had to be a metaphor there somewhere, but he didn't have enough brainpower or energy to think of it.

Ignoring his leg, Isaiah rigged his gear, grateful for the pack that had fallen ahead of him and well out of Zach's reach. Without the climbing gear in the pack, he had no chance.

Even with it he feared he had no chance. Why did he care if he survived, when he'd failed Heidi and left her in Zach's hands? He'd wanted to be a hero to redeem his past, but it was so much more than that. His past didn't matter. He didn't matter.

What mattered was Heidi.

He almost chuckled to himself. Who did he think he was to elevate himself to the role of Heidi's hero? She could take care of herself, and he'd bet right at this moment the woman had taken control of the situation. He let that image urge him on because any other visions about what could be happening to her would crush him where he was.

He assembled his gear to rappel deeper into the crevasse, toward the light. Adam and David had explored ice caves and crevasses and all manner of glacier features, and though the wonders had always intrigued Isaiah, he'd never made the time to explore with them, always busy with his own endeavors. Maybe it was more that he felt like an outsider to the Warren family. He wanted to be one of them, but given his lie to them about who he really was, that hope was as dead as he would be if he didn't climb out of the abyss.

But if given another chance, he'd go with them. He'd take Heidi to explore, too. Do everything, and take every opportunity. A near-death experience went a long way to making a person want to slow down and take the time to see God's creation.

Finally near the bottom of the crevasse, Isaiah lowered himself the rest of the way, keeping his gear on, and took a few breaths to calm his heart, steady his focus away from his injured leg. He looked up at the wall of ice he'd just descended and wondered how in the world he'd done it with a damaged body.

God, I know You hold me in the palm of Your hand. I never doubted that. But right now, I'm struggling... Isaiah choked up. Couldn't finish his prayer, even though it was silent.

Lord, please. I pray for Heidi and for Cade and even Rhea. Protect them and save them, and if I'm blessed enough to make it out of here, then maybe I can right some wrongs.

He let his gaze follow the light again and, looking up, saw the way out. He'd have to climb. Squeezing his eyes shut, Isaiah pictured Heidi's smiling face back before all the drama. Back before he'd hurt her. If he ever had the chance to be with her, he would never hurt her again. But he reminded himself that he'd revealed everything. He doubted she would have him now.

Isaiah drew in a long, measured breath, gutted it up and half crawled, half climbed out of the crevasse. As he neared the source of the light—the small entrance to a hole in the ice—he figured he had just enough energy to make it through.

And after that?

Only God knew.

In the tunnel, he felt the cold air whipping around him already, accompanied by snow. That meant the storm would bear down on the ice field soon if it wasn't already. Isaiah would be lost forever, buried alive, if he stayed tucked away in the crevasse, but crawling out into the storm to die from exposure didn't seem like much of a choice, either.

Peering below him, his heart sank. He'd burned all his energy and couldn't make it all the way back down if he wanted to. He was almost out of the chasm. His only choice was to keep going and hope for the best.

Pulling his broken body out of the entrance to the ice cave, Isaiah fell flat against the snow, gasping for breath. In the distance, he heard helicopter rotors, growing stronger.

Louder.

Isaiah sat up the best he could and waved his arms. A coast guard helicopter hovered above him. Nothing had ever looked so good.

That is, until the rescuers hoisted him into the helicopter, and he saw Heidi—smiling and crying at the same time.

Careful of his leg, Heidi wrapped her arms around him and hugged him close and tight. It felt incredible. He hesitated for a millisecond, then hugged her back, drawing in the scent of her hair. They held each other long and hard. He didn't want to let go.

Then his eyes drifted to that ominous green bag.

Heidi had never been more grateful for anything in her life than the moment she'd spotted

Isaiah in the snow waving. She wasn't ready for him to loosen his arms around her, but she knew he had to be in pain.

Then he gripped her shoulders, a fierce look in his eyes. Not at all the look she wanted or expected. Isaiah had gazed at her with regret and with such longing right before he'd fallen into the crevasse. She wanted to see that in his eyes again. He'd told her that he loved her. Had he forgotten? Was it all a lie?

"How did you survive?" she asked, a sob in her words. "I thought you were dead, but I had to look for you. I had to hope."

He ran his thumb down her cheek. "I'm glad you did, Heidi. Thank you. I thought I was gone, too. I would have been if you hadn't come when you did. Hadn't shown them where to look."

Heidi closed her eyes, savoring the comfort and reassurance in his touch.

"I found a way out of the crevasse and followed it."

Her eyes blinked open. "With a broken leg? You have serious survival instincts."

His grin wiped away the earlier scowl. "I thought about you, Heidi. I had to get back to you. Why don't you tell me what happened? How did you escape?"

Heidi shifted in the seat. "It's a long story. I'll tell you everything later. I promise." She didn't want to ruin this moment by sharing her tactics. Nor did she want to think about that look that had skewered her when she held the gun on Zach. She couldn't shake it. Couldn't shake the feeling that he would be back. Changing the subject was a good idea.

"They found Cade," she said. "He's going to be all right. Rhea, too. They transported her to a hospital and she's in the ICU, I think." Heidi leaned closer so she wouldn't have to yell over the steady whir of the helicopter. "I hear she's telling them everything, after the way Zach treated her."

"How do you know all this?"

"Cade, I talked to Cade. David told us that you ending your radio call with 'over and out' clued him in and the search for us was on. But with the storms and being shorthanded on teams, it took them a while to find us. So good job."

"I'm glad to hear that, Heidi."

"When they found Cade, he told them where to look for us. Where Zach had us guide him."

"Did they also capture Zach and Jason? The pilot?"

She shrugged. "I don't think so. I haven't heard." He was back to that again.

"Did you tell Cade everything?"

Pursing her lips, she shrank back. "What are you talking about?"

Isaiah's gaze slid to the green bag on the floor then back to her, the scowl returning. "I think you know. Why is the money bag in this helicopter, Heidi? What have you done?"

Heidi blew out a breath. "Can't you be happy that we are all alive? Who cares about what's in that bag? You can't think that I took it for myself."

His grin softened the intense displeasure in his eyes, but only to a point. "Funny thing. While I was crawling out of the crevasse, I pictured you escaping all by yourself. You're strong and brave and shrewd. I figured you'd get the men out of the way. Remove me, the hero wannabe, and you'd take Zach down all by yourself. Looks like I wasn't far off. So what *did* happen?"

She hadn't wanted to tell this story more than once, and she knew she'd have to tell it to the authorities. "I wanted to get back at Zach for taking everyone away from me. He made me pack the bags on the plane and I stowed this one in the snow beneath the plane. When he wasn't looking, I took the gun from his pocket before he ever knew what happened. Told the pilot to let me out and take off or I would kill Zach. He and Jason agreed they didn't need me."

Admiration brimmed in his gaze, but only for a moment. Isaiah shook his head, and then an expression of anguish crossed his face. The medic tried to administer a painkiller, but Isaiah refused.

"Let me see if I understand. The pilot took off without the money. None of them knew you'd taken it."

"That's right."

"But they know now."

Heidi couldn't stand Isaiah's recrimination and averted her gaze. Watched out the window and held on, praying this thing didn't crash with the winds whipping at it. Isaiah grabbed her hand, the gesture forcing her to look at him.

"Why did you do it?"

"I already told you!" Why did he have to grill her like this? "To hurt him. Besides, I couldn't overpower Zach or Jason and hold them until the authorities arrived, but at least I could rescue the money." Right. That had nothing at all to do with why she'd taken it, and by the look in his eyes, Isaiah knew it.

"You've put yourself in grave danger."

"No kidding. That was two million dollars."

His eyebrows shot up. "Two million dollars?"

"Yes. But there won't be any reason for him to come for me because I'll be turning the money over to the FBI. They're meeting us when we land. I've already given them the plane's registration number, too, so they can track these guys down quickly."

"You think Zach will know that you turned the money over to the government? If he finds out, do you think he'll care? He will want revenge."

The helicopter jerked and rolled. Heidi held fast, while Isaiah cried out in pain.

She eyed the medic. "Do something for him."

He nodded and administered a painkiller.

Heidi looked out the window again, trying to gain control over her roiling insides due to the turbulent flight. She hated seeing Isaiah in so much pain, most of it physical, but by his reaction she knew she'd caused him additional pain through her actions.

Oh, Lord, what have I done?

She'd brought the threat home with her. Not only was *she* in danger now, but her whole family.

Heidi let her gaze drift back to Isaiah. His eyes were closed, agony still etched on his face. He was a brave, courageous man, just like she'd always thought he was. But he'd run away from his problems, lied about who he really was. Heidi understood him better now.

The irony. Heidi might have to do the exact same thing in order to keep her family safe. She

might have to look over her shoulder for the rest
of her life, watching out for the day Zach would
come for her.

TWENTY-ONE

Like two bodyguards, Cade and David escorted her from the FBI's satellite office in Juneau. She and Cade had both shared their stories about the ordeal more times than she could count, as if they were the criminals. Heidi had been questioned more than either of the men because she'd taken the money right out from under Zach's watchful gaze.

Heat swam up her neck as she reiterated how she'd drawn his attention away from his money. In the end, the FBI was grateful the money had been returned and appreciative of all the information the SAR team shared about Zach and his partners-in-crime. The hunt for them was on.

She climbed into Cade's truck after the boat ride from Juneau, sitting between him and David. Their longtime friend and bush pilot, Billy, usually flew them in his float plane, but he was in the Alaska bush today, so they'd taken the boat, which took much too long, in her opinion. Regardless, the ordeal was finally over and she had thought it would never end. In truth, she'd never been sure they would survive, and it seemed a little surreal to be sitting next to Cade. The rest of the world continued on— life as usual—and hadn't come to a screeching halt just because the three of them had been abducted.

But something was missing for Heidi. Or rather, someone. Isaiah had been taken to the hospital to be treated for his injuries and had been questioned there.

"Have you heard anything more about Isaiah? Is he going to be all right?" Heidi didn't dare look at Cade. She understood now why Cade had cautioned her to avoid Isaiah, but he was being a little hard on the guy.

"He's fine."

She was still working through her feelings on Isaiah's past, but that didn't mean she didn't care for him fiercely. And that was putting it mildly. She had wanted to go directly to the hospital and see him, but Cade and David insisted on getting back home. Grandma Katy and Leah were waiting.

"Did they release him?"

"Not yet." David shifted in the seat next to her. "But don't worry about him. He can take care of himself. Adam is there with him. They'll return to Mountain Cove together."

"We need to get home," Cade said.

Heidi didn't argue with Cade on that one. She knew that Leah had to be anxious to tell him about her news if she had some. Heidi hated that she knew there was a possibility that Leah was pregnant and hadn't said a word to him, but it was Leah's place to share, not Heidi's. Cade drove his truck into the driveway of the home they shared with Grandma Katy and everyone climbed out. Cade ushered Heidi to the door as if she was a child. This was getting old.

Once inside, Heidi breathed in the aroma of Italian food mingling with that of a few baked goods. Grandma Katy appeared from the kitchen and hugged Heidi and Cade. Leah, too, but she remained in Cade's arms.

Tears streaming from her face, Grandma Katy didn't seem to want to let go of Heidi, but she relinquished her hold anyway. Gripping Heidi's shoulders, she looked her up and down. Then pressed her palms against Heidi's cheeks. "I'm so thankful God saved you, Heidi."

Then she did the same to Cade, after Leah stepped out of his arms. Heidi never doubted that her grandmother cherished and loved them. And she regretted taking the money now. She never wanted to bring harm to this house.

They'd already known that kind of fear with Leah's stalker.

Grandma Katy swiped at her tears, a broad smile on her face. "You must be hungry for a hot meal. The food will be ready in half an hour. Gives you time to clean up."

She went back to the kitchen.

Heidi decided she and David should leave Cade and Leah alone. Give them some space. She was surprised they didn't head back to their apartment.

"I think I'll run upstairs and take a quick shower." If Heidi could lie in her own bed and rest a little, that would make her day.

The next thing she knew, she woke up. She'd gotten her wish. She'd lain on her bed for a moment. She thought she'd only briefly closed her eyes, but looking at the clock, she'd slept three hours.

Climbing from the bed, she quickly showered.

She'd missed Grandma Katy's meal. Heidi shook off the grogginess and slipped down the stairs. Just as she reached the bottom step, someone knocked on the front door. She made her way to the foyer where Cade had already opened it.

Leaning on crutches, Isaiah stood in the door frame, filling it out with his sturdy form. Heidi had the urge to rush to him, much as Leah had done with Cade before, but with her disapproving brother looking on, she held back.

Isaiah's dark gaze slid from Cade to Heidi and he stepped inside. Cade offered him a seat in the living room but Isaiah declined. He moved to stand directly in front of Heidi. His proximity tugged at her, and she thought she could sense he wanted to hold her, but Cade's brooding stare hovered just over Isaiah's shoulder. She wanted to tell Cade to go away and give her and Isaiah privacy, just like she'd done for Cade and Leah.

She focused back on Isaiah and searched his eyes, remembering that awful moment right before Zach shoved him into the crevasse. She recalled the words he'd said.

I'm sorry that I couldn't get us out of this, Heidi. I love you. I think I always have.

Had he meant those words? Or had he said them because he thought he would die? Crazy thoughts. Heidi wanted the words to be true, but she still held on to other words he'd said about changing his name. About someone he loved being murdered.

Who are you really, Isaiah?

An invisible, unscalable wall stood between them. As the technical climber on the team, she knew everything about climbing. If only this were the kind of wall she knew how to climb.

"Why don't I see agents sitting in their car outside?" he asked. "Bodyguards next to the door. Law enforcement of some type watching the house, Cade? David?"

He asked the questions, but his eyes remained on Heidi. They were two people meant to be together but circumstances and life anchored them far apart.

"The FBI and their profiler didn't see Zach as likely to come to Mountain Cove. Heidi doesn't have the money anyway."

"Zach doesn't know that, does he?" Isaiah's expression revealed his exhaustion and he finally moved to the living room and carefully positioned himself in a chair. His leg in a cast, he rested it to the side.

Heidi followed him. She wanted to reach out to him and comfort him, but it wasn't her place, and with his foul mood, she doubted he would receive it. Doubted Cade would allow it. He tried to watch over her like an overprotective father. Even Dad, when he was alive, hadn't treated her like this. Even their oldest brother, David, didn't act this way. To be fair, she was closest to Cade, for some reason. And he appeared to want to protect her from Isaiah, and Isaiah wanted to protect her from an actual bad guy.

She huffed.

The men in her life.

Isaiah squeezed the bridge of his nose. "You have to know your sister is in danger. What are we going to do to protect her?"

"I'm right here in the room, boys. No need to talk about me like I'm not here. I can take care of myself, so you don't need to watch out for me."

With her statement both men, who'd been staring each other down, turned to her. David entered the living room munching on a chocolate chip cookie. He looked at her, too.

Someone rang the doorbell and walked right in without waiting. Adam hurried into the living room. "I let Isaiah out close so he wouldn't have to walk so far, then parked at the curb."

Great, now Adam could stare at her, too.

"You guys sure had us worried." He hugged Cade and then Heidi. He squeezed Isaiah's shoulder. "Not to downplay the severity of your injuries, but good thing a broken leg was all you got out of this nightmare. You could have all been killed."

"Does no one but me understand this isn't over yet?" Isaiah knocked his crutches over. "Heidi took Zach's money. He's coming here for Heidi. Whether or not she has the money, she's in danger."

David put his hands on his hips. "I understand."

"Why'd you take the money, Heidi?" Cade asked.

"To right a wrong, okay?"

He blew out a breath. Funny that her brothers' ire didn't bother her nearly as much as Isaiah's.

But she was frustrated with him, too. She wanted to ask him what it felt like to be a person of interest in a murder investigation. What had it felt like to love someone who was committed to another? How could she love a man like that after everything she'd been through? Correction, she already knew she loved him with every fiber of her being, but how could she *be* with him?

"You brought the danger to everyone, not just yourself," Leah said. She knew that better than anyone because she'd done that same thing to Cade's family. She'd led a killer right to this house. And if Leah was pregnant she had even more reason to be concerned.

"Fine. I'll pack my junk and leave."

Heidi whirled and stomped away.
Cade started after her.

"No, Cade. Let me." Isaiah attempted to stand. Not so easy with his leg.

Adam handed Isaiah the crutches he'd knocked over. He really wanted to punch a hole in a wall. He climbed to his feet, surprised to see Cade hadn't followed after Heidi. David either.

When Isaiah had a good grip on the crutches, he started toward the stairs. Oh. Stairs. He frowned.

"I'm going after her," Cade said. "Someone needs to talk some sense into her."

"Cade," Leah said. "Let Isaiah do this."

"I agree," David said.

Thanks for the support. Isaiah didn't want to complicate things with Cade, so said nothing at all. He eyed the stairs. He could do this. He left one of the crutches behind and used the rail on his right side for support.

"Isaiah." Cade stepped into view. "I appreciate what you did for my sister. I know you did the best you could, and you probably saved her in ways we'll never know. And if you can actually make it up those stairs, I bet she'll be willing to listen to whatever you have to say."

Cade's nod of assurance was all the confidence Isaiah needed. It was a form of permission. At least that's how Isaiah saw it. Cade finally trusting him again. He maneuvered his way up the stairs and was near exhaustion by the time he got there. He'd have to work his strength back up. Adam appeared behind him on the stairs and handed him the crutch he'd tossed.

Isaiah moved down the hallway, looking for Heidi's room. Sure enough, she was packing her bags. When she looked up and saw Isaiah standing there with his crutches, her eyes widened.

"What are you doing?"

"What does it look like? I came up here to talk to you."

Heidi shut her suitcase. "About what? I've made up my mind. There's no talking me out of this. I made a mistake and I'm not going to sit around and wait for Zach to show up."

"My sentiments exactly." Isaiah moved all the way into the room. "I hadn't planned to sit around and do nothing, so I came up with a plan."

Heidi's wary expression wasn't what he expected. He almost changed his mind. He'd told her that he loved her. But obviously, she didn't return his feelings. That was okay. He'd never thought he deserved her love. But he would do this for her. Protect her, the only way he knew how. He would protect the woman he loved this time if it was the last thing he did.

"Come back with me to Montana. My family has a ranch. You can stay there." And he wanted to see his family to tell them again how sorry he was for all the pain he'd caused. Just like Heidi, he wanted to right a wrong. "You can stay there until the authorities catch him, if you want. And maybe I can even convince you that I'm a good guy, after all." Oops, he hadn't meant to say that out loud.

She stared up at him from where she sat on the bed, next to her luggage. "I don't know, Isaiah. I'm so confused. I need time to think things through."

Isaiah leaned against the doorjamb. "About us?"

"About us. I mean if you're taking me to Montana in hopes—"

"No, I'm not." The pain her words caused grew in his throat, and he could barely speak. "I'm doing this to protect you."

Suddenly Heidi stood from the bed and she moved closer to him. She pressed her hand against his chest. His heart. And he knew she had to feel his heart pounding at her touch.

"I...don't believe you."

"It doesn't matter if you don't return my feelings. I'll protect you." She was right. Deep inside, if he didn't lie to himself, a small part of him hoped that he could love her and she would return his love. That nothing that had happened would stand in their way this time.

"Who said I don't have feelings for you? It's more about trust. I don't even know who you are."

"All the more reason to come to Montana with me and find out. I understand why you need someone you can trust, and maybe I can be that person for you."

Thinking of the one kiss they'd shared in the most awkward of places, he lifted his hand, pressing it against her cheek. Heidi closed her eyes, and Isaiah kissed her again. Oh, yeah, somehow he had to convince her he was one of the good guys. But what he feared most was that the price would be too high and he would fail again.

TWENTY-TWO

Heidi strolled with Isaiah toward Mountain Cove's small float-plane dock, where they would board the aircraft that would take them to Juneau. No airports or security checks here. They'd face that in Juneau. From there they would fly to Seattle and then on to Montana. Seeing the plane in the distance made her palms sweat. She was really going to do this.

Heidi had said her goodbyes to Grandma Katy, David and Adam. Cade and Leah had driven Heidi and Isaiah to the dock. But now the whole idea seemed surreal.

She gasped and paused, and Cade, walking behind her, nearly ran into her. He caught her elbow and turned her to face him. In the corner of her vision, she saw Isaiah stop and lower his bags to the ground. But he didn't approach them.

"What's wrong?" Cade asked.

"I'm worried about everyone's safety. Are you

sure this is the right thing to do?" She'd never lived anywhere else except during her college years. This had been her home forever.

"You're in good hands with Isaiah. Put some distance between you and Zach, and wait it out on Isaiah's family's ranch. You're okay with that, aren't you?"

Heidi was relieved that Cade had gotten over his trust issues with Isaiah. "I'm not worried about Isaiah. This will be the perfect chance for me to get to know him better." And she wanted that, didn't she? She'd almost lost him once before and now she was getting a second chance to see what might happen between them. But going to Montana was about much more than that. It was about running away and hiding from some killer who might never show up.

Isaiah stood next to Cade now. "It's your choice, Heidi. I just thought if you went away you would be out of danger."

"I know. I think this is for the best." *As long as Zach doesn't track me down there.*

She'd been such a bad judge of character too many times, and she'd made a poor judgment call when she'd taken the bag of money.

Cade and Leah walked with them the rest of the way until Heidi finally turned and hugged her brother. "I'm so excited that I'm going to be an aunt soon. I'm thrilled for you and Leah, Cade."

Oh, God, please keep them safe. She was doing this for them as much as anyone. She couldn't stand to worry about Leah and the baby and the chance Zach would show up to harm them. Next, Heidi hugged her sister-in-law.

Leah squeezed her hard. "This is all going to work out. You'll see. And remember, the FBI will catch Zach, and all because of the details you guys shared with them."

Heidi nodded and waved goodbye to them. Sucking in a deep breath, she and Isaiah walked the length of the dock to the float plane sitting in the water.

The pilot came around to assist with their luggage. Heidi didn't recognize him. Usually Billy flew them to Juneau. Maybe he'd been busy this time.

When he stood upright and faced them, the air whooshed from Heidi's lungs.

"Zach," she whispered.

He pointed a gun at her. "I came back for my money."

"I don't have it. I turned it over to the FBI."

"Unfortunately, I believe you. If I can't have my money, then I want you. But I can't trust you, can I?"

In a flash, Isaiah threw himself in front of her, gunfire splitting her eardrums.

"No!" The scream tore from her lungs.

On the dock, she held a bleeding Isaiah. Around her, men wrestled Zach to the ground. Heidi didn't care about any of that. Isaiah blinked up at her, his eyes out of focus.

Oh, God, please, don't let Isaiah die. Tears streamed down her face.

She'd had a second chance with him and she'd thrown it away because she'd been too afraid to trust. "Oh, Isaiah, I'm so sorry. I've been such a fool to hold back my love from you. I know who you are and your past doesn't matter. That's how God looks at us, so who am I to hold that over your head?"

His eyes closed.

Heidi held him tighter. "Stay with me. Stay in the land of the living, please. I…love you. I think I always have."

Though his eyes remained shut, he grinned at that. Her heart skipped.

"Why did it have to take me almost losing you again to be willing to love? I'm ready now, to risk my heart and my life again. So you have to be all right."

Isaiah opened his eyes and looked at her, all pretense stripped away. She saw nothing but love. "The price was worth it."

"What are you talking about?"

"I knew it would cost me something to convince you I'm one of the good guys."

"I've always known you were a good guy. You didn't have to take a bullet for me."

"Oh, but I did."

Then it was over. Isaiah closed his eyes.

Isaiah woke up to bright white surroundings and the smell of a sterile environment.

A heaviness he couldn't shake clung to his thoughts and he blinked a few times to remember where he was. He was in a hospital. That much was obvious.

Someone moved from the chair on his right and was at his side, squeezing his hand.

Heidi.

She smiled at him, ran her hand down his face. Man, that felt good. Maybe he should stay right here in this hospital bed, though he wouldn't want to keep aching all over like he did at the moment.

Cade stepped into the room, followed by David and Adam. Leah lingered against the back wall with Heidi's grandmother.

"You're a real trouper, you know that?" Cade said. "You took a bullet for Heidi. You saved her. I knew I could trust you to keep her safe."

Isaiah scraped a hand down his face. "What about Zach?"

"They got him," Heidi said. "Jason wasn't too far away so they snagged him, too. Not sure about the pilot, but Zach was just crazy enough to come back. I don't know what would have happened if you hadn't been there."

Cade moved in closer. "Just want you to know how glad we are that you made it. You're one of us. You're like a brother to me."

"And me." Adam nodded.

"And me." David crossed his arms.

"I'm not going to say you're like a brother to me, I'm sorry." Heidi laughed.

Isaiah's heart was full. How could they know that's all he ever wanted? To feel as if he was one of them. "You guys are too good to me. I always wanted to be part of a family of heroes." Part of the Warren family. That more than made up for the mistakes of his past.

"And you were the hero this time." Leah winked at him from across the room.

"But I want to know why you're not going to tell me I'm like a brother." Isaiah's grin nearly hurt his face.

"Um, could you guys give us a moment?" Heidi eyed her siblings.

They chuckled and filed from the room.

"This is why." Heidi leaned in and kissed Isaiah thoroughly, holding nothing of her feelings back this time. And he pulled her closer, wanting to give her his whole heart.

He tried to ignore the pain in his side and leg,

but Heidi must have sensed his discomfort and eased away. "Well, if I can't think of you as a sister, what about if I think of you as my wife?"

Her eyes widened.

Isaiah feared he'd messed up. This wasn't exactly romantic. "I'm not trying to take advantage of the fact that I took a bullet for you, I'm just simply looking at the facts. I've loved you for how long now? Three years going on four? And if you feel the same way, what are we waiting for?"

She flashed him the most beautiful smile he'd ever seen, and he was glad to be the one to put it there. He hoped to put many more of those on her face.

"How could I possibly refuse the man that I love? A man I know I can trust with my heart and with my life? How could I not take a chance on you? There is nothing that would make me happier in this world than to be your wife."

* * * * *

Dear Reader,

I hope you enjoyed reading *Untraceable*. What a wild ride that was to write. I also hope you took a moment to research and look up a few images of the real places I included in the story, like Devil's Paw and Michael's Sword springing from the Juneau Icefield. Perhaps you perused a few images of the blue ice of a crevasse. If you did, I'm sure you were left with a sense of awe at God's glorious and amazing creation.

As you can tell, I enjoy putting my characters through the wringer in man-versus-nature and man-versus-man stories. But the truth is, even in our not-so-harsh everyday lives, we can struggle with emotional and spiritual dark places in a very physical way. The battle to survive and keep pushing on rages around us and in us. Both Heidi and Isaiah were strong Christians and held to their faith, but even then they both struggled spiritually in very tangible ways. My hope is that in some way you can relate to either Heidi's or Isaiah's struggle to deal with the issues that arose from their pasts. The struggle to know that God was with them. He is with us during the very real everyday issues that are alive and well in our own lives, and try to knock us down into dark places.

As Christians we can struggle with the need to know and feel that God is here with us, and we might feel untraceable—that even God has lost us. But in the end, we find out that He was here all along.

Psalm 139 says it so much better, but no matter how far away from Him we might travel—either physically, emotionally, or spiritually—He is always here. I pray that you sense His presence in your life today!

As always, I love to hear from my readers. You can contact me via my website at elizabethgoddard.com.

Many blessings to you.
Elizabeth Goddard

LARGER-PRINT BOOKS!

GET 2 FREE LARGER-PRINT NOVELS PLUS 2 FREE MYSTERY GIFTS

Love Inspired®

Larger-print novels are now available...

LILPDIR13R

REQUEST YOUR FREE BOOKS!
2 FREE WHOLESOME ROMANCE NOVELS
IN LARGER PRINT
PLUS 2
FREE
MYSTERY GIFTS

⁂⁂⁂⁂⁂⁂⁂⁂⁂⁂⁂⁂⁂⁂⁂⁂⁂⁂⁂⁂⁂

HEARTWARMING™

⁂⁂⁂⁂⁂⁂⁂⁂⁂⁂⁂⁂⁂⁂⁂⁂⁂⁂⁂⁂⁂⁂⁂

Wholesome, tender romances

YES! Please send me 2 FREE Harlequin® Heartwarming Larger-Print novels and my 2 FREE mystery gifts (gifts worth about $10). After receiving them, if I don't wish to receive any more books, I can return the shipping statement marked "cancel." If I don't cancel, I will receive 4 brand-new larger-print novels every month and be billed just $4.99 per book in the U.S. or $5.74 per book in Canada. That's a savings of at least 23% off the cover price. It's quite a bargain! Shipping and handling is just 50¢ per book in the U.S. and 75¢ per book in Canada.* I understand that accepting the 2 free books and gifts places me under no obligation to buy anything. I can always return a shipment and cancel at any time. Even if I never buy another book, the two free books and gifts are mine to keep forever.

161/361 IDN F47N

Name _____ (PLEASE PRINT)

Address _____ Apt. #

City _____ State/Prov. _____ Zip/Postal Code

Signature (if under 18, a parent or guardian must sign)

Mail to the **Harlequin® Reader Service:**
IN U.S.A.: P.O. Box 1867, Buffalo, NY 14240-1867
IN CANADA: P.O. Box 609, Fort Erie, Ontario L2A 5X3

* Terms and prices subject to change without notice. Prices do not include applicable taxes. Sales tax applicable in N.Y. Canadian residents will be charged applicable taxes. Offer not valid in Quebec. This offer is limited to one order per household. Not valid for current subscribers to Harlequin Heartwarming larger-print books. All orders subject to credit approval. Credit or debit balances in a customer's account(s) may be offset by any other outstanding balance owed by or to the customer. Please allow 4 to 6 weeks for delivery. Offer available while quantities last.

Your Privacy—The Harlequin® Reader Service is committed to protecting your privacy. Our Privacy Policy is available online at www.ReaderService.com or upon request from the Harlequin Reader Service.

We make a portion of our mailing list available to reputable third parties that offer products we believe may interest you. If you prefer that we not exchange your name with third parties, or if you wish to clarify or modify your communication preferences, please visit us at www.ReaderService.com/consumerschoice or write to us at Harlequin Reader Service Preference Service, P.O. Box 9062, Buffalo, NY 14269. Include your complete name and address.

HWDIR13R